Portland Midwives

From rivalry to romance!

Dedicated midwives and best friends Hazel and
Bria cofounded and run the Multnomah Falls
Women's Health Center in Portland, Oregon.
Their holistic approach brings moms-to-be from
far and wide. But they're ruffling a couple of
feathers over at the local St. Raymond's Hospital…

That is, before all that friction turns into
flirtation…and these two midwives discover that
the miracle of love is just as powerful as
the miracle of life!

Read Hazel's story in
The Doctor She Should Resist
by Amy Ruttan

Discover Bria's story in
The Midwife from His Past
by Julie Danvers

Both available now!

Dear Reader,

Thank you for picking up a copy of Hazel and Caleb's story, *The Doctor She Should Resist*.

I was completely thrilled when I was asked to write a duet with Julie Danvers. I'm always honored to work with a fellow author.

We came up with two best friends who open a birthing center in Portland.

Hazel has a fiery temper, and when a greedy board of directors tries to shut down the birthing center, she's not going to let anyone stand in her way. Not even the broody, handsome head of obstetrics, Dr. Caleb Norris.

Caleb has no problem with the birthing center. Since his wife died eighteen years ago, he's kept his head down and done his work. That's until he meets Hazel Rees and the sparks begin to fly as they both work together and find love.

I hope you enjoy Hazel and Caleb's story.

I love hearing from readers, so please drop by my website, www.amyruttan.com, or give me a shout on Twitter, @ruttanamy.

With warmest wishes,

Amy Ruttan

THE DOCTOR
SHE SHOULD RESIST

———

AMY RUTTAN

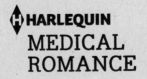

HARLEQUIN

MEDICAL
ROMANCE

HARLEQUIN®
MEDICAL ROMANCE™

Recycling programs for this product may not exist in your area.

ISBN-13: 978-1-335-40931-7

The Doctor She Should Resist

Harlequin Enterprises ULC
22 Adelaide St. West, 41st Floor
Toronto, Ontario M5H 4E3, Canada
www.Harlequin.com

Printed in U.S.A.

Born and raised just outside Toronto, Ontario, **Amy Ruttan** fled the big city to settle down with the country boy of her dreams. After the birth of her second child, Amy was lucky enough to realize her lifelong dream of becoming a romance author. When she's not furiously typing away at her computer, she's mom to three wonderful children, who use her as a personal taxi and chef.

Books by Amy Ruttan

Harlequin Medical Romance

Caribbean Island Hospital

Reunited with Her Surgeon Boss
A Ring for His Pregnant Midwife

First Response

Pregnant with the Paramedic's Baby

Cinderellas to Royal Brides

Royal Doc's Secret Heir

Baby Bombshell for the Doctor Prince
Reunited with Her Hot-Shot Surgeon
A Reunion, a Wedding, a Family
Twin Surprise for the Baby Doctor
Falling for the Billionaire Doc
Falling for His Runaway Nurse

Visit the Author Profile page
at Harlequin.com for more titles.

To my amazing friends, who encouraged me these last couple of months.
Your support means so much to me.

**Praise for
Amy Ruttan**

"*Baby Bombshell for the Doctor Prince* is an emotional swoon-worthy romance…. Author Amy Ruttan beautifully brought these two characters together, making them move towards their happy ever after. Highly recommended for all readers of romance."

—*Goodreads*

PROLOGUE

HAZEL REES WAS FURIOUS, but she was trying to keep it under control. This was not St. Raymond's fault, rather it was the doing of a greedy board of directors.

She knew how they all worked.

When she and her best friend, Bria, had applied to open their birthing center across from St. Raymond's hospital, the chief of staff, Dr. Victor Anderson, had been so supportive.

Then the city planning commission had slapped them with a whole bunch of red tape, which had delayed them.

And the reason?

St. Raymond's board of directors had *concerns* about the Multnomah Falls Women's Health Center even existing. Not the staff of the hospital, just the board, and Hazel knew that the new chairman of the board, Timothy Russell, had friends at city hall.

Politicians were corrupt, as far as she was concerned, but she and Bria had come too far now to let anyone stand in their way. This whole thing was ridiculous.

It was a complete waste of time, and now they were here at this tribunal to see if the city would even approve of them opening at all. Their reason was some idea about being in direct competition with the hospital, because it was apparent that the hospital's bottom line was more important to the board of directors than providing great health care to Portland's pregnant women.

As far as Hazel was concerned, why else would they be here?

All the work on their birthing center had just stopped, and they were forced to plead their case in front of the city commissioner.

Bria reached out and squeezed her hand, as if sensing she was angry.

Bria was far calmer than she was.

Which made sense.

Hazel's father had always said she had rather a fiery temperament. She had never believed him, until now, sitting here, waiting for the hospital representative to come in and give their report.

On what, exactly, she didn't know.

All she knew was that the hospital representative was late.

Which ticked her off all the more.

The door opened.

"Sorry I'm late," a male voice said.

Hazel turned and was taken aback by the gorgeous, albeit frazzled-looking man who'd walked into the tribunal room.

He was probably the most handsome man Hazel had ever laid eyes on.

He had a mop of well-tamed dark brown curls, with a sexy bit of silver at the temples. The well-tailored and expensive suit he was wearing showed off an impressive set of broad shoulders. There was an air of dignity around him and she wasn't quite sure what it was, but he made her heart go pitter-patter.

It had been some time since she was so instantly attracted to a man.

Not since Mark, in fact.

She thought she'd learned from that terrible mistake. She tried not to look at the man, but she couldn't help herself.

What was wrong with her? She needed to focus.

Get ahold of yourself. You're in a crucial meeting!

"I take it you're the representative from the hospital?" the meditator inquired.

"Yes. I'm Dr. Caleb Norris, the head of obstetrics at St. Raymond's."

Bria glanced at Hazel and leaned over. "I thought Dr. Anderson was the head of obstetrics?" she whispered.

"No. He's the chief of staff. The head of obstetrics wouldn't speak to us before because he was too busy."

So this was the man who had no time to speak to them, according to his secretary and his residents.

Seems he had found time to speak *against* them, though!

"And you are here on the hospital's behalf, Dr. Norris?" the mediator asked again, for the record.

He nodded. "Yes. The board of directors said you required facts, and I have the data necessary for your inquiry relating to births in this area and in the state."

"By all means, Dr. Norris," the mediator said.

"Thank you." Dr. Norris pulled out a chair and took a seat at the table, right across from Hazel.

Their gazes met; his blue-gray eyes pierced her to her very soul. It caused her stomach to do a flip, but she folded her hands carefully and straightened her spine, meeting his cool look with a lift of her eyebrow.

His eyes widened, as if surprised to see her. And there was suddenly a spark, a twinkle warming his gaze that made her cheeks heat and a zing of electricity flow through her. Like she had been struck by something.

Focus. Keep calm.

He looked away, clearing his throat as he shuffled papers.

"Dr. Norris?" the mediator asked.

"Yes. Sorry." Caleb put down the papers. "I lost my train of thought there for a moment."

Hazel smiled in satisfaction that he seemed to be a bit discombobulated by her.

Good.

It would bode well in their favor if he struggled to get his point across.

"My board of directors asked me to tell you the percentages of births, etcetera, that come through

St. Raymond's and why our hospital is vital to the area and can more than handle the needs of the community."

"Our midwife clinic is also vital," Hazel interrupted hotly.

Bria grabbed her wrist as if to silence her.

Dr. Norris's eyes narrowed as he glared at her.

"Yes, I am already aware of your projected figures," the mediator stated. "I am interested in Dr. Norris's facts, his proven figures, if you please, Ms. Rees. Yours are not fact yet."

Hazel subsided and nodded. "Of course. My apologies."

"Dr. Norris, please continue," the mediator said.

"Thank you." Caleb stacked his papers. "Last year we had eight maternal deaths, two hundred and eleven infant deaths, and there were one hundred and thirty-eight neonatal births and one hundred and fifty fetal deaths. That is, of course, in the whole county, not just St. Raymond's. Out of forty thousand births in the state, the county had nine hundred live births, and four thousand patients came through our doors. Multnomah is a large county. We do see the majority of the state's births, but there are other hospitals and other midwives in this county."

"Thank you, Dr. Norris," the mediator said. "There's a lot to consider and to take to city planning. We'll adjourn and meet again in two weeks."

Hazel was fuming, but she got up and left the

tribunal room. Everything was going to be delayed again.

It was so frustrating.

She followed Bria outside.

"Why didn't they bring in a midwife with an established clinic too?" Bria asked. "The mediator said our numbers weren't fact yet, but an established midwife would have those proven numbers."

"Why didn't they ask a pregnant woman about her comfort of care either?" Hazel groused. "You and I both know there's a huge demand in this area of the city. A lot of women don't want a hospital birth."

"Some women don't have a choice," a stern voice said behind her.

Bria took a step back to answer a phone call that came through, so Hazel was alone to fight this battle against Dr. Norris and she crossed her arms. "I'm well aware of that. Still, it would have been good to have had a pregnant woman's perspective. As head of obstetrics, I would think you, of all people, would agree."

"I do agree, as it happens, but the board of directors simply asked me to present the figures and I have done so."

"Births are more than just data," Hazel said, bristling.

His blue-gray eyes narrowed. "Look, I'm not your enemy."

"No, but you represent people who wish to deny

women access to having a choice in their health care. Not all women want a clinical birth. Some prefer a more holistic approach."

"Hardly denying access."

"Our center opening is being delayed, thus you're denying access."

"And as I've already explained to you, that isn't my fault. I will not stand here and continue this discussion, Ms. Rees. I have patients to see. Good day."

He turned to walk away.

Hazel scowled.

Why did the good-looking ones always have to be so stubborn and so prideful? So prickly.

She only hoped that when this all blew over, when their birthing center finally opened, she could work with Dr. Norris if she had to.

Right now, she wasn't so sure she could.

That fiery temper her father always teased her about suddenly kicked in as she glared at his retreating figure. It took a lot for her to keep her cool, especially when she was so passionate about something and the center was her and Bria's whole world.

She couldn't let him walk away.

Hazel might regret it, but as they were opening their center across from St. Raymond's, she planned on working with him in the future. Therefore, this discussion was far from over.

She marched after Dr. Norris and darted in front of him.

His eyes widened in shock again, as if no one had ever confronted him before.

"Madam, please..."

"No, I don't think we're quite done talking about this."

"I beg to differ."

Hazel cocked her eyebrow. "Do you now? Well, I beg to differ too."

A small, brief smile quirked his lips and his eyes narrowed. "Is that so?"

"We're going to have to work together."

"Are we?" he asked. "I thought you were opening a birthing center not starting a job at St. Raymond's."

"You're being a bit pedantic." She was so infuriated with him, and she had to keep reminding herself that it was all for the benefit of the center, finally realizing Bria's and her dream. She could deal with the likes of Dr. Caleb Norris for that.

Can you?

"*I* am being pedantic? I thought our discussion was over. As I said, I have patients to see. I'm a very busy man."

"Yes, you made that very evident when Bria and I came to speak with you. Your secretary made it quite clear when you wouldn't even deign to grace us with your presence."

"As I have stated, I have a lot to do…" He tried to sidestep her, but she was having none of that.

"You're not the only one who has better things to do, Dr. Norris. Do you have any concept of what you've done here today?"

He looked confused. "I presented the facts and figures that my hospital's board of directors asked me to. What's wrong with that?"

"They're the ones who are trying to stop us from opening," Hazel said, hoping she wouldn't burst out crying, which was what she always did when she got as angry as she currently was.

"I don't think that's what happened here. Your center will open."

"It's being continually delayed. Your report today, your lack of willingness to confer with us so we could explain things to you has done irreparable damage. Do you even care about women's health at all?"

There was a flash of pain across his face and Hazel flinched, cursing her temper under her breath. She didn't mean to attack him like that, and she instantly regretted it.

"That was unfair," she said. "I know that you do care…"

"Yes," he said absently. He wasn't looking at her, but she could see the hurt still etched in his face and the air of vulnerability that suddenly cloaked him, and she couldn't help but wonder why he was so pained.

That's not your business.

"Our birthing center will give women more choice, which can only be a good thing," she said calmly.

"I understand." His eyes were cold now, and he could barely look at her. "You do understand my information was not a personal attack on your center, don't you? I was merely doing my job."

"I get that," she said with a sigh.

"You would do well to do the same, Ms. Rees. As you say, we'll most likely have to work together in the future. Perhaps, for now, we should go our separate ways before we say anything else we might regret."

"Agreed, but Bria and I could really use your support. It would be nice to know that you respect a woman's right to choose her own health care."

His lips pressed together in a firm line. "I always do respect that decision, but what I wonder is, will you accept that same choice?"

"What do you mean?"

"If a woman chooses to have a, as you put it, clinical birth, will you stand by her decision? Will you stand in the way of the hospital doing its job?"

Hazel crossed her arms. "I'm kind of insulted you are insinuating that, Dr. Norris."

"Tit for tat, Ms. Rees. You assumed the same of me."

Damn. He had a good point.

"No, I wouldn't stand in the way. I meant what

I said. I want us to be able to work together in the future."

He smiled, slightly, but she could tell that his feathers were a bit ruffled still. "That remains to be seen. Good day, Ms. Rees. Again."

This time she didn't try to stop him. She stepped to the side and watched him walk away. She had overstepped her bounds a bit and she regretted it, but there was a lot at stake here.

She and Bria had worked so hard.

What she had to do now was swallow her own hurt pride, her temper, and just focus on the next steps to get their center approved and opened. She had to believe that the board of directors at St. Raymond's wouldn't keep trying to put a stop to it, even though there was a part of her that was worried they would.

But one could live in hope, right?

CHAPTER ONE

Six months later

DON'T TURN AROUND. *He's staring at you again.*

Hazel Rees could feel that she was being watched. Ever since she and Bria had decided to open the Multnomah Falls Women's Health Center, Hazel felt like she was under complete scrutiny from the board of directors from the hospital across the road. Especially at that tribunal where they'd sent their head of obstetrics to delay their building permits.

Although, Dr. Caleb Norris hadn't known what the actual agenda of the board of directors was. He'd just been doing his job presenting figures as requested. The members of the board of directors weren't medical people, and they only cared about money. The chairman of the board was particularly devious. Hazel could tell, just by his actions. Whatever Caleb claimed, Timothy Russell definitely wanted to ruin their center.

It's because you're a threat to their bottom line.

And that fleeting thought made Hazel smile to herself. She liked being a threat. Especially after the hospital board had delayed them so many times by going to the city.

St. Raymond's birthing hospital had had the

monopoly on births in this area for far too long. There was a huge need for a birthing center here, and that's what she and Bria had provided. Both of them were certified midwives, and Hazel was also a nurse practitioner. She wanted to offer not just an amazing, safe birth experience, but also provide postpartum support for years afterward. Hazel had seen the difficulties her sister had experienced after her C-sections, how her sister's adhesions after surgery had left her with pelvic floor problems and pain. Hazel had grand plans to help women with their whole health.

This had been her and Bria's dream since they'd met during midwifery training. Hazel usually kept people at a distance, but somehow Bria had weaseled her way through her defenses and they'd become fast friends with the same goals.

It had been a fight to get here, but they were here now and Hazel couldn't be more proud if she tried. Delays hadn't stopped them from what they had managed to achieve so far.

Even if the head of obstetrics, the surly, brooding Dr. Caleb Norris, grumped at her all the time. Hazel hated that she was so attracted to a man who had apparently taken it upon himself to become her sworn enemy.

Enemy was probably too strong a word, but ever since they'd met at the tribunal every single time she saw that man they got into an argument over the most foolish things.

He was intelligent.

Incredibly professional.

He seemed so put together too. Caleb made her weak in the knees, but then he would open his mouth and it would go downhill from there.

Always sniping at one another.

He grated on her nerves.

They were on the same side in the grand scheme of things, yet when she was around him her temper got riled up. He was just so infuriating!

There was a part of her that wanted him to just take her in his arms and kiss her. Then she recalled the hurt look on his face during the tribunal and the feeling she'd got that she'd wounded him in a particularly vulnerable place. Maybe he was broken and needed love? But that instinctive need to heal had got her into trouble before, and she'd ended up in a very bad relationship because of it.

Mark had been a man she thought she could heal with love. He was a surgeon she'd met at hospital after completing her nurse practitioner training. He'd been jilted practically at the altar, and he'd told her that's why he'd pushed her away when they first met, but that in the end, he couldn't resist her.

It was like something out of a romance novel.

He'd driven her crazy too, at first. Then came the passion. She'd thought his heart had finally been mended, by her. That she had helped him over the pain and hurt of being so cruelly jilted. But after she'd let her guard down, and once he was firmly planted in her heart, then he'd betrayed her trust by cheating on her.

It was then she'd learned his ex-fiancée had left Mark because he had cheated on her too.

Hazel had also discovered that everyone they'd worked with had known the truth all along.

They had been watching the drama, gossiping, predicting when Mark would do the same to her. And they were right. She'd been made to look like a complete fool.

It had broken her.

Completely.

What she needed to do now was listen to the logical part of her brain. The one that was telling her that Dr. Caleb Norris would probably be just like Mark, and she needed to keep him squarely where she put him, which was on her "do not resuscitate" list. She wasn't going to put her heart on the line again for a vulnerable-looking man.

Or any man, really.

She laughed to herself thinking about how foolish she was to be so attracted to another brooding, wounded doctor. She certainly had a type, didn't she? She didn't know what had caused the look on Caleb's face that day at the tribunal, and although she still felt bad about it, it certainly wasn't her business.

She tucked back a loose strand of hair that had escaped her braid and glanced over her shoulder at the hospital across the street. The large, looming, multimillion-dollar birthing hospital that seemed to have a revolving door policy when it came to babies and women's health.

When she and Bria had researched a location, they'd picked a spot across from St. Raymond's because it was a stellar hospital with a good reputation.

The chief of staff was welcoming.

It was a good fit.

It was beneficial to the community.

Then politics from the board of directors had reared its ugly head and delayed them.

It was certainly a facility like St. Raymond's that had dealt with her sister so quickly. The Arizona hospital had shuffled Hazel's older sister and niece out of the door so fast just because her sister didn't have the best insurance.

Then her sister had hemorrhaged, and she'd almost died.

It was at that moment Hazel decided to pursue midwifery once her nursing training was complete, and her dream had been to open a birthing center. One that wouldn't push women through a revolving door. A center that would see a woman through the entire journey, right into postpartum care and beyond, and to help those women who couldn't always afford to pay.

Health care needed to be equal access for all. Not just for a select few.

Lack of funds, lack of insurance that decided

who received the best health care put lives in jeopardy. Like what had almost happened to her sister. The thought of losing her had utterly terrified Hazel.

It had been one of the worst moments of her life. That and Mark's betrayal.

An ache filled her chest, and she shook those painful memories away. That was all in the past. Her sister was healthy. Her niece was seven and thriving. She'd moved on from Mark. Everything was good.

She was here now to help those who needed her, and it didn't matter to her that the big bad wolf's house was just across the road. Or that the wolf in question was standing outside hospital's main entrance, his hands in his pockets, scowling at her as usual.

Hazel raised her hand and waved politely.

"Hello, Dr. Norris. Beautiful day, isn't it?" she called out breezily.

Caleb looked away and she couldn't help but smile. She didn't know what it was about her that irked him so much. She'd apologized for upsetting him, but it didn't seem to matter to Caleb. Nor, so she'd told herself, did she care. The problem was, she really did. Still, no matter how many brooding glares he sent in her direction, he wasn't going to alter her course. They were here to stay.

Hazel pulled out her keys and saw out of the corner of her eye that Caleb was headed her way.

Damn.

What did he want now?

She turned to face him, trying to plaster the fake smile on her face that she had recently mastered whenever she had to deal with him. Her jaw was beginning to ache at how much she had to clench it around him. Bria always warned her to play nice, and she'd do it to keep her friend happy.

"Dr. Norris, to what do I owe the pleasure of your company?" she asked through gritted teeth.

"You called me over," he said tersely. "I abhor shouting."

"I didn't call you over," she responded dryly. "I greeted you, instead of ignoring you."

"Yes, you greeted me by shouting across the street like…"

"A fishwife?" she asked when he seemed temporarily lost for words.

"A what?"

"Something my grandfather always said. He was from Cornwall."

Caleb's lips pressed together in a firm line at her rambling. "I deduced that you wanted to speak with me, since you took the time to shout across the street."

"No. I really didn't need to speak with you. I'm sorry for exchanging pleasantries. I'll remember that for next time and just ignore you." She turned to try and end the conversation, but he stepped in her path. Just like she had done to him six months ago. She braced herself for an argument, but instead he looked like he was struggling to say something.

Like he didn't want to say whatever it was he was thinking and her stomach twisted in a knot, expecting the worst.

This was so not how she wanted to start her day.

"Actually, I do need your assistance," he finally said in a lowered voice, as though imparting a scandalous piece of gossip.

Hazel took a step back and cocked an eyebrow. "You what?"

Caleb's own jaw tightened. "I said I need your help."

Hazel couldn't quite believe what she was hearing. Since their little run-in, Caleb had largely kept his distance and mostly dealt with Bria, whom he didn't fight with. Bria was definitely more of a balm when it came to dealing with the staff at St. Raymond's, so Hazel let her be the voice of reason over there.

There was just no talking to the man. Hazel had tried, but he reminded her of every pompous jackass she had dealt with when she had been studying to be a nurse. And he was just as emotionally closed off as Mark had been. He was everything that Hazel didn't want. She wasn't getting involved with a man who was clearly lugging a lot of baggage.

He drove her completely bonkers and yet she was highly attracted to him.

She had a problem.

A serious problem.

And now, here he was, two months after their triumphant opening, and he was asking for her help.

"Do my ears deceive me or are you asking *me* for help?"

"Don't make this harder than it already is," he said tightly. "Will you do it or not?"

"It depends on what it is. If it's to help you figure out a way to shut down our health center, then I'm going to have to decline."

Caleb rolled his eyes. "Hardly. I've told you repeatedly that I was merely presenting the facts that the board of directors asked me to."

She knew that, but did he have to be so grumpy about it? Or maybe it was just her who brought it out in him?

"Fine. Still, you usually go to Bria. You don't usually talk to me."

"She's more logical," he remarked.

Hazel cocked her head to the side. "Is she? Then speak with her."

"She's not available."

"I'm busy too."

Caleb sighed and pinched the bridge of his nose. "Please, Ms. Rees, can we just have a normal conversation?"

She sighed. "Of course."

"Thank you." He looked at her with his gorgeous blue-gray eyes. The color reminded her of the sea when a storm came in. Cool, yet mysterious and dangerous with hidden depths.

She felt she could get lost in them, if they weren't attached to someone as annoying as him. As she stared up at the man, his eyes narrowed and went a bit flinty, and she couldn't help but wonder what it would be like if he smiled.

He was such a handsome man. His dark brown hair, cut short on the sides, but with a curl on top, was streaked with a little silver to match that on his temples, but it so suited him. His white lab coat, his tailored pants and polished shoes made his athletic six-foot-one build look pristine.

Everything about him gave off an air of a put together, well-to-do man, and she had no doubt that if this were Regency times he would be polishing his hessian boots with champagne.

He exuded power and control.

Whereas she was a bit of a mess, but she liked being that way. More down to earth, comfortable and approachable for her patients. She was pretty sure she was all the things that annoyed Caleb greatly.

Which was a shame.

She couldn't help but wonder what it would take to get Caleb to loosen up a bit. To see him smile. To kiss him.

You've trodden down this path before. Don't make the same mistake again.

Mark had been broody, untouchable.

Intelligent and charming.

She'd been like putty in his hands and he knew it. He'd woven a web of lies so easily about being heartbroken. She'd felt like she'd connected so deeply with Mark. Like they were soul mates.

She'd been such a fool.

Men like Mark didn't have a shred of empathy. She didn't know Caleb well, but she'd bet her money on him being exactly like her ex. It was apparent he was hiding a deep hurt of some sort, but she had no desire to find out what it was.

She had her heart to protect.

Caleb was off-limits.

Hazel blew that thought away, hoping that the heat she felt from her fleeting, ridiculous musings wasn't creeping up her neck for the whole world to see.

"Look," he said, breaking through her introspection. "I'm not here to bandy words with you. I need your help. I have a patient I'd like to bring to you. One that wants a midwife's opinion on a vaginal birth after caesarean."

"Of course. When?"

"In about an hour or so if that's all right?" he asked.

"Sure."

Caleb nodded. "I'll see you then."

He didn't thank her, but just left as abruptly as he'd arrived, marching back across the street to the hospital with his white lab coat fluttering behind him. Hazel shook her head, still slightly stunned over the exchange that had just taken place between them. Why hadn't he simply called and booked the appointment with their receptionist, Joan?

There was no point in trying to figure him out. Hazel didn't have time to waste on the intricacies of Caleb's mind, though there was a part of her that really wanted to. He was just the kind of man she always fell for.

And therein lay the rub.

She just didn't trust her own judgment around men like him. And she certainly couldn't trust again; her heart couldn't handle another betrayal like that. When she'd walked away from Mark, she'd sworn never to get seriously involved with anyone ever again.

She had plans.

Romance and love were not in those plans.

The universe had made it perfectly clear she should steer clear of love and focus on her career.

She headed into their clinic and Bria was already there, going through files at the main desk.

"Hey," Bria said brightly. "I didn't think that you were coming in so early."

"I couldn't keep myself away. And apparently I now have a patient to see."

Bria cocked an eyebrow. "Oh, really? Who?"

"Dr. Norris is bringing her over in an hour. A consult about a vaginal birth after a caesarean."

Bria leaned forward. "Oh, that sounds kind of intriguing."

"Why?"

"The broody obstetrician that you constantly butt heads with is bringing you a patient. You, the proverbial thorn in his side."

Hazel chuckled softly. "I suppose it is kind of like the opening of a book club type of novel."

"They could so make a movie!" Bria teased.

"Noted." Hazel picked up a blank patient file and poured herself a cup of coffee. "If he comes barging in, just point him to my office."

Bria nodded. "Will do."

Hazel headed to her office, set her bag and the file down, and took a sip of her coffee. She was expecting a busy day, but she'd hoped her morning would be quiet so she could go over inventory and prep for later.

Instead, she was catering to Caleb.

Except that she wasn't. She had to put it out of her mind that this was about him. She was helping someone in need. And if it was a woman in need, she didn't care if the woman was the devil's wife.

There was a knock.

"Come in," Hazel said, trying not to sigh as she set down her coffee, knowing full well that it would be cold by the time she got back to it.

Joan stuck her head around the door. "Good morning! A walk-in patient has come in. Can you see her?"

"Sure. If Dr. Norris comes with his patient, just ask him to wait."

Joan eyes widened. "Dr. Norris?"

"Yeah."

"Coming to see you?"

Hazel laughed softly. "Yes. I know. It caught me off guard too."

Joan smiled. "Sure. No problem."

Hazel got up and walked out into the waiting room. There was a nervous young woman sitting there. She had long blond hair and was twisting the hem of her T-shirt. A backpack was at her feet, and she was tapping her leg.

Joan handed her the intake form.

"Lizzie?" Hazel asked.

The young woman looked up. "Yes."

"I'm Hazel. It's nice to meet you."

They shook hands. Lizzie was trembling.

"Nice to meet you, Hazel," she said. "Thank you for seeing me so quickly."

"Not a problem. How about we go into my office?"

Lizzie nodded and Hazel led her into her office. The young woman took a seat, and Hazel shut the door so they had privacy. Lizzie was wringing the hem of her shirt again.

"How can I help you?"

Lizzie swallowed hard. "I had... I'm late. I'm usually pretty on time with my cycle, but my period's about two weeks late."

"I see. Have you taken a pregnancy test?"

"No." Lizzie blushed.

"Are you underage?" Hazel asked, although if Lizzie were, she could be lying about her birthdate. Not that it mattered. She wouldn't deny this young woman care. Still, if she was underage, she would have to get Lizzie's parents involved.

"No. I'm eighteen," Lizzie said. She worried her bottom lip. "I just didn't want to go to my regular doctor. He's friends with my dad and…"

"It's okay. We can do a test here."

Lizzie looked visibly relieved. "Thanks."

"I'm curious. Why not go to the hospital across the road?"

"My father works there."

"Ah, I see." Hazel got up and opened the door to the bathroom. "There are sterile bottles. I'll need a sample, and then I can do a test."

Lizzie nodded. "Okay."

She disappeared into the bathroom and Hazel sighed.

Eighteen.

So young.

Her own mother had been eighteen when her brother was born, and she knew how tough it had been for her parents to make ends meet. She knew how much her mother had to give up to take care of them all.

Lizzie came out of the bathroom, and Hazel

took the sample into the center's testing room. She placed a strip into the bottle and waited.

The strip confirmed it.

Lizzie was pregnant.

Hazel headed back into her office. Lizzie was tapping her leg again, her blue-gray eyes wide as she looked up at her.

"You're pregnant. When was the first day of your last period?" Hazel asked, sitting back down across from her.

"The twenty-first. As I said, I'm two weeks late and pretty much regular."

"So you're about five weeks, then."

"Yeah." Lizzie sighed.

"What're your plans?" Hazel asked gently.

"I would like to keep the baby. The father, my boyfriend—we're planning to get married after college."

"Okay. You might have to put college on hold at some point and tell your parents."

"I'm eighteen and an adult. I don't have to tell my dad yet."

"I know, but they may notice a bump when you go home at Christmas," Hazel said.

Lizzie smiled. "I'm from Portland, but you're right. I live with my dad. He'll notice for sure."

"If your dad won't be supportive, can you stay with your mother?" Hazel asked, assuming that her parents were divorced because Lizzie kept talking about her father only.

"No," Lizzie said quietly. "My mother died when I was born."

Hazel's cheeks heated. "Oh. I'm so sorry."

"It's okay. I'll tell my dad…when I'm ready. You won't tell him, will you?"

"No. Patient confidentiality. I won't be making that call," Hazel assured her.

Lizzie smiled, relieved. "Good."

"Shall we determine a due date? It's too early to do an ultrasound, but we can talk about when that will happen as well. That's if you would like to stay under my care and if you want me to be there for the birth of your child."

"Yes. I would much rather have my baby here. My dad would like me to go to medical school, but I've always been fascinated by midwifery and would much rather deliver here than a hospital."

Hazel nodded. "And you're in college you say?"

"Bachelor of Health Science, to appease my father, then midwifery after I get my bachelor."

Hazel didn't want to remind her that her career plans might change slightly with having a baby, it wasn't her place. Lizzie seemed smart enough to know what she was taking on.

She was of legal age. She didn't need to keep drilling it into her that her life would become so much more complicated with a newborn baby and college to deal with.

Hazel was not her mother.

She took down Lizzie's health information and

figured out the baby's due date. The baby was due to arrive early next year. In January.

After Hazel had set up the next appointment, she got up to walk Lizzie out. As they left her office, a loud male voice boomed across the waiting room.

"Lizzie?"

The young woman groaned. "Hi, Dad."

Hazel spun around and saw Caleb, frowning and confused. Then it hit her.

Lizzie was Caleb's daughter?

He had an eighteen-year-old child? And Lizzie had said her mother had died when she was born… so he was a widower.

Hazel couldn't help but wonder what had happened to his wife. It explained why he was so closed off. The pain of losing the woman you loved must be unbearable. She felt bad for him. It also solidified her resolve to not get any closer to him.

It was way too complicated.

Caleb came over. "What're you doing here, Lizzie?"

"She's interested in midwifery, so we were talking about that," Hazel said quickly.

He frowned, crossing his arms and looking at Lizzie. "Is this true?"

"Y-yes," Lizzie stammered. "Th-that's it. Hazel was so kind to let me know what training was needed and how long it takes to become a certified midwife. Jeez, why else would I be here, Dad?"

Caleb didn't look convinced. "You're sure you're not pregnant? That boy you're dating… I swear…"

"Derek's not a boy, Dad! He's the same age as me. He's in college too. Could you keep it down? You're embarrassing me," Lizzie hissed.

"Fine. We'll talk about this later."

Lizzie rolled her eyes and turned back. "Thanks again, Hazel, for being so reasonable, unlike some people I know."

Hazel bit back a chuckle as Caleb watched his daughter leave, looking flabbergasted.

"You're early," Hazel remarked. "And here without a patient I see."

"She's on her way. I thought we could talk about her case before she arrives."

"Of course." Hazel stepped aside so he could enter her office.

She hated keeping such a secret from Caleb, because he had the right to know he was going to be a grandfather, but that also wasn't her place as Lizzie's midwife. Lizzie had to be the one to tell her father.

She was still a bit shocked he had an eighteen-year-old daughter. All right, he had a touch of gray, but he certainly wasn't over forty. He couldn't be, but all of what Lizzie said about not wanting her father to find out made complete sense to her now.

If her dad was an obstetrician like Caleb, he would definitely be spouting off his disapproval.

Hazel had seen it enough in other parents of teenage children. And she was certain raising a child on his own and becoming a surgeon hadn't been easy, so he wouldn't want that for Lizzie as well.

However, what she needed to do was take care of Lizzie and not get involved in anything beyond personal care for her patient. It was most definitely not her business what happened between Caleb and his daughter, unless it affected Lizzie's or her baby's health.

Caleb sat down in Hazel's office still a bit distracted by the fact that he'd just seen Lizzie here.

She said she's not pregnant.

And he believed her. Lizzie had never lied to him before.

For the last eighteen years, he had been trying to hold it all together, and not always very successfully in his opinion. Most days, he felt like a complete failure when it came to Lizzie. One time they had been extremely close, but then she'd hit the teenage years and something had changed.

He knew, biologically, what had shifted in his relationship with his daughter. She was a grown woman now. She was self-reliant and really didn't need him anymore. He was no longer the center of her world.

Her boyfriend, Derek, was.

He'd seen it happen to other parents; he just

didn't know how to deal with it himself. He was frozen, and it felt like his world was spinning out of control.

Lizzie was very like his late wife, Jane, in so many ways.

Same temperament.

Same drive.

Same expressions.

Jane had got pregnant when she was young and he was still in medical school. At the time, he'd been thrilled. He and Jane had felt like they could do anything. She'd left school so that she could stay home to raise Lizzie.

Everything would be okay.

Then Jane had died, and he'd had both medical school and a newborn to cope with. With so much to juggle, he'd just done the best he could to get through each day.

Seeing Lizzie here had scared him.

She'd only just started college.

He didn't want Lizzie to give up her schooling like Jane had done—that had been Jane's choice, but Lizzie wanted other things. And he painfully remembered his days of interning while parenting a young child. It was brutally hard.

She says she's not pregnant.

Still, he couldn't calm his nerves. There had been a lot on his mind lately, and this just added to the unrest. Most of his thoughts during the last six months had centered around a certain midwife at the new birthing center across the road and how he could best avoid her.

Except now here he was. In her office.

Hazel was one of the most fiery, intelligent, attractive, stubborn women he'd ever met. That day he'd walked into the tribunal had changed his life.

He could not stop thinking about her.

He'd gone to present facts about birth rates in the county. He'd genuinely had no idea the board of directors was trying to prevent the birthing center from opening. He'd been so taken aback when he'd discovered that, and he knew that he had probably ruined any chance he might have had with Hazel.

It had been a long time since he'd been so attracted to another woman.

Then Hazel had opened her mouth and infuriated him by jumping to conclusions about him.

It was like he'd been hit with a bolt of lightning.

He'd been mesmerized by her.

If he wasn't a single dad trying to keep his life together, if he wasn't so afraid of getting his heart obliterated again, he suspected he'd already be pursuing Hazel Rees.

But it was clear she didn't particularly like him, and he'd been out of the dating game for far too long to even think about starting up a relationship with a woman like her.

What would a young, vivacious woman want with a middle-aged father of a young adult anyway?

He cocked his head, staring at her as she talked. He could never find the right words to say.

She was one of the most beautiful women that he'd seen in a long time. Hazel had this rich auburn hair, with a slight curl. Her hair was untamed, just like her spirit. The dark brown eyes were keen and her heart-shaped lips were quick to deliver a barb.

She was an intellectual challenge, just as much as she was beautiful.

And Caleb wanted to get to know her further.

It unnerved him how much he wanted to get to know her.

How much he liked her.

He had to remind himself that she was off-limits. He didn't have the space for her in his life. It was better for his heart to be alone.

He had his work and his daughter. That's all he needed.

Is it, though?

"So you wanted to talk about your patient?" Hazel asked, shutting the door.

"Yes." Caleb cleared his throat. "She's pregnant with her second. She's a new patient. Her first baby was delivered in California via caesarean section. They, my patient and her husband, just moved here from Oxnard. She would like to try for a vaginal birth after caesarean and would like a midwife to consult."

"And what's so strange about that?" Hazel asked, sitting across from him.

"I didn't say it was strange," he snapped. "Why are you constantly putting words in my mouth?"

"Usually obstetricians that I've dealt with in the past are wary of a vaginal birth after caesarean. So I assumed…"

"You assumed incorrectly. Again."

She lowered her eyes. "I'm sorry. Please continue."

He was taken aback. She'd never apologized before. What had changed?

She eyed him curiously. "Why are you looking at me like I have antlers or something?"

"I've just never heard you apologize before."

She laughed softly. "Bria said I have to be nicer to you."

"Well, I appreciate the apology. Thank you."

"You're welcome."

He narrowed his eyes. "Lizzie told you about my late wife, didn't she?"

"She did."

"I don't need your pity if that's why you're apologizing."

"I'm not pitying you," she said quickly.

"Oh, no?"

"No," she replied gently. Her dark eyes held a soft gleam, and he found he quite liked this side of her.

"I appreciate that. Often I get pitying comments.

My late wife died eighteen years ago. I think I'm doing okay by now. I've had enough of the sympathy, and I feel like it's insincere sometimes."

"Of course. You raised a smart young woman, by the way," Hazel stated.

"Thank you. It was difficult, I won't lie. I was in medical school when she was born and interning during the toddler years, trying to become an OB/GYN. Day care cost a fortune. Raising a baby alone is incredibly hard for anyone."

"You didn't have help?" Hazel asked.

"No. My parents were both gone as were my late wife's. It was just me and Lizzie."

Although, as Lizzie grew older, she didn't need him anymore. Not as much. Lizzie was the one encouraging him to move on and find someone, but he just didn't have the time or the inclination.

He always had Lizzie as an excuse not to date or get serious with anyone.

There was nothing stopping him now, except himself and his fear of losing someone else he loved. Whoever coined that phrase about it being better to have loved and lost than never having loved at all was so wrong.

The pain of loss felt like it had swallowed all the love fully.

"So why don't we talk about your patient and how I can help," Hazel suggested.

He smiled in relief. "I'd like that."

He was glad to return the talk to business.
Business was safe.
Emotions never were.

CHAPTER TWO

ALL HAZEL WANTED to do was focus on work with Caleb, but it was hard to concentrate on just that when he was so close and she could drink in the spicy, clean scent of him. Then her brain started wandering, wondering what kind of cologne he used or was that just him.

Hospitals were usually scent free.

Seriously. You need to focus, she chastised herself yet again.

She took a discreet step back as he gave her the particulars of the patient. She made her brain concentrate on the facts and the figures that he was presenting, rather than how good he looked or how great he smelled.

The last time she'd had such an intense physical reaction like this to a man was with Mark, and her heart didn't have to remind her what had happened in that situation. How he had completely obliterated her trust and humiliated her.

The memory began to unfurl in her head, and she couldn't stop it.

She'd been bursting with good news because she had got into the midwifery course of her choice, and she was so excited to be starting that journey.

Mark was a surgeon, and he had been the one to tell her to pursue her dreams of becoming a midwife. She had been saving up for the course and paying off her nursing course debt since they met.

She'd wanted to share with him how she had got a scholarship, but when she'd gone to the ward where she'd known he would be working, he was nowhere to be found.

It had been kind of odd.

Mark had lived for work, and the ward was really busy.

So she'd asked the charge nurse if she'd seen him.

"No. I haven't seen him lately. The last I saw him he was heading with his surgical fellow to the intensive care unit to check on a patient. I'm sorry I can't be of more help, Hazel."

Hazel smiled. "No worries. I'll just go and see if I can catch him on the way back from the ICU."

She headed down the hall that was used for staff only.

A group of interns sniggered by a closet door.

"What's going on?" Hazel asked.

The interns tried to regain their composure. "A couple is having sex in the supply closet. We tried to go in to get suture trays to restock, but the door is jammed."

Hazel frowned. "They shouldn't be in there."

"At least let them finish," an intern joked.

"It's unsanitary," Hazel groused. She knocked several times, but no-one answered. Finally, she grabbed a pen from one of the interns and applied

the old trick her father had taught her to jimmy open a door. With an easy pop, the door swung open and her whole world toppled over when she saw Mark, with his pants down, and behind his body, pressed against the wall, his surgical fellow, Melody.

"Hazel?"

She heard shocked gasps and a snigger of laughter behind her. Tears stung her eyes, tears of rage and humiliation, as she slammed the door and ran off...

Hazel shook the painful scenario from her mind.

She hated it when those old memories came back to haunt her. She had thought, in the last six years since it happened, that she'd firmly locked them away. That she had put them in their place, but apparently not.

"What do you think?" Caleb asked, intruding on her morose thoughts.

"Sorry, what?"

He looked slightly annoyed, pursing his lips. "I asked you if you think she's a good candidate?"

Hazel stared down at the facts and figures. It was all just numbers. Their patient was a good candidate. Her last caesarean section was a low transverse incision. She didn't have any other previous complications, and her latest ultrasound showed that the placenta was in a good position with the baby down.

"I don't see why not. I haven't met her or examined her, but I would like to do that and I could go from there."

"What do mean, go from there?" Caleb asked dubiously.

"Using my instincts. Facts and figures are great, Dr. Norris, but sometimes there are things you can't predict."

He looked utterly crestfallen for one moment. "Yes. I'm very well aware of that."

And she knew then that she had intruded into the memories of what must have happened to his late wife. Not that Hazel knew exactly what had happened, only that she had died when Lizzie was born.

"I don't see why she can't attempt a vaginal birth this time. What I'm saying is that I would feel more comfortable if she did it in a birthing suite in the hospital."

Caleb cocked an eyebrow. "Really? You're suggesting she gives birth in the hospital?"

"Why do you sound so surprised?"

"I just figured that since you want to get to know the patient and go with your instincts, that you would want her to give birth here in this homey environment and not at a sterile hospital. Not that this place isn't sterile like a hospital, it's just…it's not so bleak. The decor makes it more comfortable."

She frowned. "Hospitals have their place. I am a nurse practitioner as well, you know. I worked in a hospital for a couple of years. And since this is a vaginal birth after caesarean section with a patient that neither one of us is familiar with, my instinct tells me that it would be better if she delivered in a birthing suite with access to an obstetrical team that can give her a repeat C-section if needed."

"That makes sense."

"Now you really sound surprised," Hazel teased.

"Well, the few times I actually try to strike up a rational, logical conversation with you we seem to always end up at cross-purposes."

"That's not my fault," she responded swiftly.

He chuckled. "Oh, it so is."

"What?" she asked, feeling kind of affronted.

"You have a temper."

"I don't!"

Only she knew she did. Her father said it came from his grandmother who was Irish and Scottish. Hazel didn't really believe that; her father was military and she knew that it came from him.

Completely.

He was just too stubborn to admit it.

Just like she was doing now.

Hazel threw up her hands. "I don't want to argue, but if the patient wants a midwife there for her, I'll be at the hospital and willing to help her in any way that I can."

"I agree. I don't want to argue, and I appreciate that you are willing to work with me. I think it would be safer for our patient if she gave birth to her child at St. Raymond's, under both our care."

"Good. I'm so glad we're in agreement."

He was laughing softly to himself.

"What?" she asked.

"In the last six months, with all our interactions since that day at the tribunal, this is the first time that we've really agreed on something."

Hazel cocked her head to the side. "I suppose it is. Don't let it go to your head. When did you say your patient is coming?"

"I thought she'd be here by now. Hold on a moment," he said as he fished his phone out of his pocket and checked it. "Ah, they've had to rearrange some things, so they're not coming right away." Caleb just shook his head. "So, I'll arrange an appointment for later, if you're free?"

"I think I am. Just check with Joan. She's the one who books in all the appointments. Of course, that appointment could be interrupted if a patient needs me."

"Of course, the same goes for me."

Hazel nodded. "I look forward to working with you, Dr. Norris."

"And I you."

He left her office, and she sat down in her chair weakly.

After that tribunal, if Hazel had been told she was going to make a deal with the devil and work with Caleb, she would've laughed in everyone's faces.

Who was laughing now?

* * *

After Caleb made the arrangement for his patient to come to his office and meet Hazel, he got called down to the operating room to do an emergency caesarean section on one of his patients. He liked being in the operating room; it cleared his mind, because he was solely focused on the work that he was doing.

And he really needed to clear his mind.

He couldn't believe that he'd asked Hazel Rees to consult on a patient with him, but this new patient had been insistent that she have a midwife attend. To add to that, the chairman of the board of directors, Timothy Russell, who Caleb detested, had insisted that Caleb do whatever he could to make this particular patient comfortable.

Apparently, her husband was wealthy and she also came from money.

Caleb knew that Timothy's agenda wasn't about the health or care of the newborn and mother, but whether he could hit them up for donations. He knew how people like Timothy thought.

It drove him crazy, but he kept his head down and focused on his work.

His work was security, and the only thing to keep him sane since his wife died. It's what had provided a living for him and Lizzie, but there was a part of him that wished he could branch out on his own, open his own practice someday.

Provide the same level of care that Hazel gave to her patients.

Sometimes, it felt a bit like a revolving door at the hospital, and he missed the human connection and interaction.

The problem with walking away from St. Raymond's and opening his own practice was the financial risk, and he wasn't sure that he wanted to risk so much on something that might fail.

Playing it safe was always better. The one time he'd played fast and loose, Jane had conceived Lizzie. Not that he ever regretted having Lizzie, but he'd lost Jane in the process.

No, it was better to stay put. To not take the risk.

Even though he had taken a huge risk to talk to Hazel over Bria. He wasn't attracted to Bria, therefore she was safe. Hazel, on the other hand, was a gorgeous ball of uncertainty.

Caleb shook those thoughts away as he scrubbed out after completing the caesarean section. What he couldn't quite believe right now was that he was going to be working with Hazel. Why was he taking the chance? Temporary insanity must be the reason.

Loneliness? Boredom? a little voice suggested.

He silenced it.

Hazel was like this tempting thing he wanted so much, but he couldn't deny he was worried about getting bitten. When they'd had their little disagreement at her office, there was a moment when he'd started to regret asking her to consult on the case, but then she completely surprised him agreeing with him.

It was the first time they had really agreed on something.

Maybe this would be a new leaf? Or an olive branch maybe?

He could only hope.

He left the scrub room and headed out onto the operating room floor. He needed to change out of his scrubs and get ready for his meeting with his new patient, Tara Jameson, and her husband, Wilfred. He had to make sure he had all his information ready for when he and Hazel consulted with them in an hour.

"Ah, Dr. Norris. I wanted to have a word with you before your meeting with the Jamesons."

Caleb froze in his tracks and groaned inwardly as he turned around to see Timothy standing there in his expensive suit.

"This is the operating room floor. You shouldn't be wearing street clothes here. It's a sterile environment."

Timothy looked nonplussed. "I'm not in the operating room."

"No, but patients pass through here. Women. Children."

"Well, I did go to your office and you weren't there."

"I was in surgery." Caleb continued to walk and

Timothy followed. He needed to lead this dunderhead away from the operating room floor and into a conference room or something so they could speak. There was an empty gallery room that was used to train residents, where they could view surgeries, but since there was no surgery in there and no residents, it was a quiet place to listen to what Timothy had to say now.

Caleb shut the door. "I'm meeting with the Jamesons soon. Is there a problem?"

"Hazel Rees. In particular her and the birthing center she opened with Bria Thomas."

"What of it?"

"The Jamesons are under the belief that she'll be attending the consult too."

"That's correct."

Timothy's eyes narrowed. "Why?"

"Because that is what the Jamesons requested, and since Hazel and Bria are the closest midwives in proximity to the hospital, they were the most logical choice."

"The Jamesons will want to have their baby at their birthing center, and that will take away revenue from us. Suppose they want to give donations to the birthing center instead of St. Raymond's?"

Caleb frowned. "So let me get this straight. You're not concerned about the medical wishes of our patients…"

"Of course I am," Timothy snarled. "Never assume that about me."

"What else am I supposed to think when you immediately talk about money?"

"Money is what pays your salary," Timothy said stonily. "Please don't forget that."

"What exactly do you mean?" Caleb asked.

Timothy turned around slowly. "What I mean is that the more money siphoned from the hospital, the less we have to pay staff. Think about that when you're inviting that Rees woman in here."

Timothy left the gallery and Caleb fumed inside.

He wouldn't forget that, but he was never going to put his patient's health at risk for money.

Never.

Hazel was pleased with how the meeting with the Jamesons and their little girl, Vanessa, had gone. She was fairly confident that Tara would be able to deliver her next baby vaginally without too much worry. The placenta was in a good place—they'd checked again at the appointment—and she was healthy, young and her scar didn't seem to be giving her too much pelvic floor trouble. And the Jamesons were very happy to have both her and Caleb working together on this.

Honestly, Hazel was glad to be working with him on this case too.

Her hands were tied when it came to surgical cases.

It was nice to have a good working relationship with him now.

At least, the start of a good professional relationship, if they could only stop arguing for long enough!

Although, she could tell that something was off about him during the consultation.

Something had clearly been bothering him. When she came over for the consult, he was even more closed off than usual and there was an air of anger in the room. Hazel was pretty sensitive to mood changes as well, and it was definitely a tense atmosphere.

"They're a lovely couple," Hazel said, trying to make conversation after the Jamesons left while Caleb was cleaning up the exam table in his office.

"Yes." His back was to her and it was stiff. His spine ramrod straight.

"Dr. Norris, are you regretting your decision to ask me here to consult?" she asked point-blank.

"No." He turned around and scrubbed a hand over his face. "I'm sorry. I had to deal with the chairman of the board just before this meeting and it's still affecting me, I suppose."

"Ah, that's Timothy, isn't it?"

"Yes."

"He's definitely not a fan of our clinic being across the road."

"No, he's not," Caleb responded. "The staff has no problem with you and Bria. I hope you know that. It's just him and his precious bottom line."

"I get that. I've worked in a hospital. I understand it."

He smiled, relieved. "Good. I'm glad, because Tara Jameson clearly wants you on this case and I do too. You can see she's close to delivering. There isn't much time to form a game plan."

"No. There isn't. Maybe we could meet tomorrow?"

"Or we could meet tonight?"

The invitation caught her completely off guard. "What?"

"You could come over for dinner. Lizzie is cooking, and I know that she loves to have company. Especially company for me so that she can sneak off and be with her friends. She always worries about me being alone."

Hazel chuckled.

She didn't know Lizzie well, but she could already tell that she was a caring girl who would be worried about her father, but Hazel wondered if Caleb knew exactly who Lizzie was sneaking off to see.

She seriously doubted that Lizzie had told her father yet that she was pregnant.

Maybe that's what Lizzie was planning on doing tonight, hence why she was cooking for him.

"I don't know…" Hazel said doubtfully.

"Is it because we really didn't get off to the best start?" he asked.

"No, it's just… I don't want to burden Lizzie. She has so much schoolwork."

"I know, but think of it as a way for us to pay you back for letting her talk to you about midwifery. As well as talking to me about Mrs. Jameson and her VBAC. It's a working slash thank-you dinner."

"Okay." She couldn't believe the words were coming out of her mouth until they did.

Did she really just agree to a dinner with Caleb? At his house?

"Great. I will email you the address, and I'll see you around seven?"

"Sure," she said. She grabbed her purse and left his office.

She walked out of the hospital a bit stunned and back to the Women's Health Center, still going over the chain of events that had just happened.

Bria walked into her as Hazel was entering the building. "Whoa, there you are. I was wondering where you got to. You look like you've seen a ghost!"

"Dr. Norris just invited me over to his place for dinner. Tonight."

Bria's mouth fell open. "You accepted? You accepted dinner at the terrible ogre's house?"

"What?"

Bria's eyes twinkled. "Don't you remember? After your first run-in with him, you were calling him the devil and an ogre."

Hazel chuckled. "He's not a terrible ogre. I was wrong. There's nothing ogreish about him."

"So you said you've accepted. Are you regretting it already?"

"No," Hazel said softly. "No, because he said it was a working dinner. And we're going to be consulting on a case, so really it's the smart thing to do. We need a good relationship with St. Raymond's in order for our center to survive."

"I was thinking of having some kind of fundraising event. It would be great to have the hospital on board," Bria said.

Hazel wrinkled her nose. "I will help, as long as I don't have to plan it. I hate those kinds of things."

Bria chuckled. "Deal. So what're you going to wear when you go over there tonight?"

Hazel felt the blood drain from her face. "What do you mean? This isn't a date, Bria."

Her friend just smiled knowingly in that annoying way she sometimes did. "Sure, sure."

"What I'm wearing is fine."

"Sure." Bria nodded.

Hazel rolled her eyes. "Get back to work."

Bria smiled again and continued on her way.

Hazel just shook her head. She could focus on the rest of her work, even though she had a bunch waiting for her. All she could think about was Caleb, and her pulse quickened. He was so prideful, so stubborn and moody, but now she understood why. He was a widower. Still hurt and grieving.

Why was she always attracted to men like that?
The wounded ones.
The broken ones.
The wrong ones.

CHAPTER THREE

CALEB'S HOUSE WAS in a posh area of Portland, and Hazel had to admit that she felt a little bit intimidated heading into this part of town. She grew up in a firmly middle to lower income family. They didn't have much, but they had enough.

Still, she was a bit overwhelmed by his wealth.

Why are you letting these thoughts bother you now?

The only thing that she could think of was that she was nervous.

That wasn't a lie.

It was nice that Caleb invited her for dinner, and she had to keep reminding herself that it was just a working dinner.

Still, his invitation had surprised her.

She should've said no, but maybe it was curiosity that propelled her to accept.

Curiosity killed the cat.

As she chuckled to herself, all the tension she was feeling melted away.

This was good.

Lizzie wasn't her only patient, but she wanted to be a midwife too, plus she and Caleb were working together on Mrs. Jameson's case. There were a lot of pros to accepting his invitation to dinner, and that's what she was going to remember.

They were colleagues now.

This dinner was a great way to get to know one another and maybe end the sniping that they had been engaged in the last six months.

Hazel took a deep, calming breath and rang the doorbell.

The door opened and Lizzie greeted her.

"Hazel! I'm so glad you made it."

"You sound surprised," Hazel joked.

"There was a part of me that wondered if Dad was pulling my leg saying you were coming to dinner and you were just saying yes to him to be nice. I was half expecting you to call him and cancel," Lizzie said excitedly as Hazel stepped inside the house and Lizzie closed the door.

In truth, Hazel had thought about that option, but didn't take it.

It was the coward's way out and she didn't want to disappoint Lizzie, who had opened up to her. She wanted to earn the young woman's trust so that she could help her.

Lizzie would need her help and support until she told her father the truth about why she had been at Hazel's clinic.

"Hazel would never do that. She's too kind. Annoying, but kind." She looked up and saw Caleb standing at the top of the stairs, leaning casually over the banister.

He was smiling as he said it, so it was meant as a gentle tease.

"I'm not the only annoying one," Hazel quipped.

"True."

Caleb came down the spiral staircase in the foyer. Her heart skipped a beat. He was wearing a V-neck sweater in a deep navy that brought out the color of his eyes, and she was surprised to see him in jeans.

She'd never pictured him as a denim kind of person.

Of course, in all her interactions with him he'd been dressed in a suit and a white lab coat.

She hadn't even seen him in his scrubs. Hazel's cheeks heated as their gazes met. He was smiling, just slightly as he came down the stairs.

"Dad, she's hardly annoying," Lizzie interjected. "Although, you certainly can be."

Hazel chuckled as Caleb cocked an eyebrow at his daughter's muttering.

"Oh, really?" he asked his daughter.

"Where do you think I get it from?" Lizzie asked, crossing her arms.

Caleb shook his head. "Would you let our guest in?"

"Right." Lizzie ushered Hazel in. "I hope you like lasagna, Hazel."

"I love it," she said, tearing her gaze from Caleb and holding out the plastic container she'd been gripping so tightly. "I brought pie."

"Yum. Thanks. I'll take it to the kitchen." Lizzie

turned to her father. "Dad, can you be nice to our guest for one minute?"

Caleb rolled his eyes, but was still smiling. "I'm certain I can."

Lizzie nodded and left them.

Hazel was still standing in the foyer, her coat on, her boots on. The only thing missing was the pie that she had bought at a local bakery. Caleb closed the gap between them.

"I am really appreciative that you came," he said. "I didn't expect you would."

"I'm not mean. Well, I guess I am annoying, but I like your daughter. She's delightful. Unlike you," Hazel teased.

"You just don't know me yet. I'm an absolute delight."

"That remains to be seen."

"I can show you some figures," he teased.

They both laughed, and the tension instantly melted away.

Caleb smiled. "Can I take your coat?"

Hazel nodded and undid the buttons. He stepped behind her, and she was suddenly aware of how close he was. Her pulse was thundering in her ears, and she was suddenly so nervous being near him and in his home.

This man who'd got under her skin for the last little while was making her weak in the knees. She never thought she'd be here, laughing with him.

And now she was in his home and he smelled so good.

You need to get control of yourself. Remember Mark? You're not a good judge of character.

The Women's Health Center was the only thing that mattered. Their relationship had to be strictly professional.

Hazel slipped off her coat and gave it to him, then sat down to slip off her boots. As soon as the boots came off, she realized she'd forgotten to change her socks and she was wearing her rainbow-striped toe socks. The rainbow toe socks that reached up to her midcalf didn't exactly go with the casual dinner skirt and shirt she'd picked out.

She'd been planning on wearing tights.

Caleb instantly saw them and there was a twinkle in his eyes. "Those are quite the socks."

"Right. I knew I forgot something," she mumbled, embarrassed.

"There's a pocket for each toe. Doesn't that drive you slightly crazy?"

Hazel glanced down at her feet and wiggled her toes. "Nope. They're quite comfortable, which is probably why I forgot to change them."

"Well, I think they look great. Unusual, but great." He was smirking as he took her jacket to the closet and hung it up. "Would you like a drink?"

"I would love one, but maybe I should go help Lizzie?"

"No. She won't want that. This is her project, and I learned over the years not to get involved with her projects. She gets testy and says I'm interfering."

Hazel chuckled softly. "So the apple doesn't fall far from the tree, then, does it?"

Caleb laughed again. "No, I suppose it doesn't."

Hazel followed him into a formal sitting room. It was decked out with antique furniture, all dark wood, and bookcases full of leatherbound books, floor to ceiling. There was also a fireplace with a fire flickering in its hearth. It was actually kind of cozy, and she could easily spend many a rainy, cold evening curled up with a good book in here.

It looked like a den of a wealthy lawyer or doctor.

And then it struck her, Caleb was just that. Although, the books looked more for show than reading. The bookcase in her loft apartment had paperbacks with creased spines from all the times she had read her favorites over and over again.

Though lately, those had been few and far between.

She didn't have much time for reading right now. Her life was all about work.

She walked over to the big bay window and there was a large maple tree outside, with leaves softly fluttering in the rather brisk wind that had got up.

"Scotch?" Caleb asked.

"Is it though?" she asked.

He cocked an eyebrow. "Pardon?"

"I mean, is it really scotch. Scotch is only scotch if it's from Scotland. If it's from here, it's whiskey."

He glanced at the bottle. "It's from Scotland."

"Ah, then it is indeed scotch." She was rambling again. She always seemed to do that when she got nervous.

"You didn't answer my question," Caleb said.

"And what's that?"

"Would you like some?" he asked.

"No, thanks. Not keen on the stuff."

"Would you prefer a gin and tonic? The wine is being saved for dinner I'm afraid."

"A gin and tonic would be wonderful." She wandered over to one of the bookcases and stared up at all the classics. She'd taken some English literature classes in university, and she recognized some of the tomes she'd had to read.

And she remembered some of them putting her to sleep.

"Have you read many of these?" she asked.

"All of them," Caleb responded.

"Seriously?" she asked.

He nodded and handed her a highball glass with her gin and tonic in it. "I loved English literature when I was in school. So I've read all the greats. I'm a bit of a collector when it comes to first editions."

Her eyes widened. "So you're telling me this is a first edition of Mary Shelley's *Frankenstein*?"

Caleb nodded. "It is. A classic feminist piece."

A smile quirked on her lips. "And you're a feminist?"

"I am an OB/GYN."

She shrugged. "It doesn't mean you're a feminist though."

"I am. I believe in the rights of women and them having autonomy over their own choices."

She was impressed. "That's very admirable. So why are you so against the Women's Health Center then?"

He sighed. "I told you I'm not. The board asked me to present the facts, and I felt my hands were tied. I only did my job."

There was an exhaustion in his voice. She remembered how boards of hospitals could be. She knew they could be money hungry. Money was really the source of all evil. She felt bad for him.

He had so much on his plate and was now having to deal with this pressure from the board. And he also didn't know yet that his college-aged daughter was pregnant. She couldn't help but wonder how he was going to handle that.

It was a lot for any one person to deal with.

All she wanted to do was reach out and comfort him.

Only she couldn't.

She had to keep her distance.

"Well, we're there now and I hope that we can work together," she said. Although, she wasn't going to hold out too much hope. She wanted to believe that everything was going to work out all right, but she'd been disappointed before.

She'd been hurt before.

Caleb's lips pressed together in a firm line, and he was staring at his shelves of books in consternation. "I would like that."

"I would like to be able to send my clients, the ones I can't help, to you. We could have a beautiful partnership." Hazel was putting a lot on the line, but it was the truth. It was, after all, another reason why she and Bria had chosen a site across from the hospital. They wanted to be able to send their surgical cases to St. Raymond's.

It wasn't to stick it to the hospital, far from it. It was so that there was another option available for their patients. It was a safety net. That was Hazel's hope always, that their midwife clinic and St. Raymond's would work in a sort of symbiotic relationship together.

Only, that wasn't the case at the moment. The board of directors had made it clear that they didn't want to work with them. At least Caleb seemed to want to, and Dr. Anderson, the chief of staff, had also been so helpful and friendly.

"You're right," Caleb said. "I hope you know that you have my full support. My board of directors won't like that, but this is about the patients. I would gladly consult on any case, and I'll send on any patient that would prefer your midwifery services over mine. Which is why I asked you to consult on my vaginal birth after caesarean case. Mrs. Jameson's case. I sincerely respect midwifery. I hope you know that."

She was a bit taken aback and didn't know quite what to say to that. This didn't seem to be the man she's assumed he was. Only she didn't know him well enough yet to be sure. She wanted to believe he was who he appeared to be, but her trust had been broken and it was hard to take Caleb's integrity at face value.

She really wanted to believe him, but she couldn't let herself.

"Thank you, Dr. Norris," she said quietly.

He smiled, his eyes twinkling in the dim light. "Caleb."

A blush crept up into her cheeks and she couldn't stop it, even if she wanted to. "Caleb then."

"You're welcome, Hazel," he said softly.

Her heart was racing and her knees began to tremble.

"Dinner is ready!" Lizzie announced, popping her head into the room and breaking the tension that had fallen between them.

"Perfect," Caleb said, turning around. "I'm starving."

Hazel took a deep breath and followed him out of the formal sitting room. Relieved to put some distance between them and this strange whirl of emotions that he was causing.

* * *

Caleb didn't quite know what overcame him. One moment they were discussing the feminist implications of Mary Shelley's *Frankenstein*, and then the next thing he knew he was forming some kind of partnership with Hazel and fighting back the urge to pull her in his arms and kiss her.

She looked absolutely adorable in her rainbow-colored toe socks.

And then he watched as she admired his books.

There was a part of him that wanted to discuss English literature with her. Curl up in front of the fireplace and talk. That's what he and his late wife had done. They had met in English literature class in college.

Jane had loved the classics just as much as he did.

When he'd first started collecting these books, she had been the one to start giving him first editions. And she was the one who had found and tracked down the first edition of *Frankenstein* for him.

"What is it?" he asked, shaking the package.

Jane made a face. "Don't do that!"

"Is it breakable? Will it explode?" he teased.

"Just open it. Or I'll open it for you," Jane threatened.

He laughed. She always was impatient, especially when giving gifts. It was one of the most endearing things about her, and he loved teasing her.

"Maybe I'll open it later."

She jumped at the package, and he'd held it over his head as she crawled across his chest in a futile attempt to get it.

"Just open it, Caleb. Stop teasing me so much."

He grinned. "Fine. I'll open it."

He torn into the paper and been stunned at the old book wrapped in parchment paper. "Is this what I think it is?"

"Well, your essay and thesis on this book was the best in our class. It's why I fell in love with you." She leaned over and kissed him.

"Is it?"

"Your sympathy for the devil. Or, in this case, the monster, was truly inspirational. The monster is definitely misunderstood."

"You fell in love with me because I sympathized with a monster?" he asked, teasing.

Jane smiled and kissed him again. "Happy anniversary."

Caleb tucked the memory away. It was a good memory, but it was just that. He had lived in the past for far too long. When Jane died, he'd had to focus on Lizzie and his career. There was no time to grieve properly. No time to move on.

It had been easier that way.

Was it easier now?

He looked across the table to see Lizzie and Hazel laughing over something as they enjoyed their dinner. He couldn't really recall the last time

Lizzie had laughed like this. Actually, when was the last time there was this kind of mirth in his home? Probably not since Lizzie was a little girl. They loved one another dearly, but as she'd grown older she'd naturally preferred hanging out with her own friends.

It was nice to hear her giggling again. Both of them had got so busy lately, they'd barely had time to sit down and have a meal together.

He was alarmed to realize he was struggling to remember the last time they'd connected like this.

He couldn't help but smile at her joy, but there was a part of him that was worried. Any spare time he had should really be spent with Lizzie. There could be nothing between Hazel and him.

They were colleagues, and he didn't want to mix business with pleasure anyway. Even if in Hazel's case he wanted to break that rule.

It's not like she'd want you.

He was a widower with an adult daughter, and Hazel was young, vibrant, beautiful.

Hazel can be your friend.

The only problem was, he didn't just want to be Hazel's friend. The moment he'd laid eyes on her he was drawn to her, attracted to her, and the more he got to know her, the more he wanted to know. He was putting his heart in a dangerous situation.

He was going to have to try and put some distance between them. Which would be hard given they were going to be working together at times.

But it was the only way he could get over this infatuation with her.

He'd been attracted to other women before and got over it easily. He'd even had a couple of flings, but no real relationship. All he had to do was get some distance. That was the key.

Not that inviting her to dinner was helping any.

Hopefully, they wouldn't have to confer on too many cases together.

"Do you want me to get out the pie?" Caleb asked, trying to escape this happy scene so he didn't get too caught up in it. It was one that he wanted to have continue, but knew that it couldn't.

"No, Dad. This is my dinner. I'll go get it." Lizzie got up and took everyone's plates.

She disappeared into the kitchen.

And an awkward silence fell between him and Hazel. This was not part of the plan. Logically, he didn't want to be alone with her, but another part of him did.

"Would you like some more wine?" he asked, clearing his throat.

"Please." Hazel held out her glass, but wasn't exactly looking him in the eye. He hoped that he didn't make her too uncomfortable.

"So, are you from Portland?" he asked, trying to lighten the tension and make conversation.

"No. I'm not. I was born in New York. We moved around a lot. My father was in the armed forces so I've lived all over. One of the longest places we stayed was in Portland though, so I've always thought of it as home. And I did my midwifery training here, which is where I met Bria. It seemed like the perfect spot. I'm glad to be back. And you? Are you from Portland?"

"No, I'm from California. I am a West Coast native at heart, but I much prefer the mountains and forests to the city."

"Portland is quite a large city," she reminded him.

"Not as large as Los Angeles, which is where I'm from."

"I would've pegged you as a WASP from the East Coast. Somewhere like Connecticut. Old money."

Caleb frowned. "What makes you think that?"

"You're a bit…well, you're a bit stiff sometimes. I guess that's a polite way of saying it."

Caleb chuckled under his breath. "So you're saying that your first impression of me, you felt like I had a stick up my backside?"

Hazel laughed. "I guess so. You were so rigid. Aren't Californians usually more relaxed?"

"Aren't military brats rigid too?" he asked.

"We're efficient," she countered.

"So am I, but I assure you I am not a WASP. My parents were actually a bit hippyish. We had money, because my father was a movie director and my mother was an actress. Quite a big name in her heyday. She was even in a Bond movie at one point."

Hazel's eyes widened. "Are you serious?"

He nodded. "Yes. So there was a lot of Hollywood parties, and A-listers at our home. I was sent to boarding school on the East Coast. So I guess that's where I probably picked up that WASP vibe that you're feeling."

Hazel leaned in. "I'm fascinated by old Hollywood. Who came to your house? Did you go to anyone's house? Oh, my goodness, did you go to any grotto parties?"

"Hardly. I was a child, but I did attend a party once at the Black Dahlia murder house."

"What is that?"

"You don't know about the haunted Black Dahlia murder house?" he asked incredulously.

She shook her head. "No, but I do read a lot of true crime."

"You said you were fascinated by old Hollywood and you read true crime. You should know about those murders. I'm not going to tell you anymore until you've read about it yourself. Then you can ask me questions, but needless to say, that was really old Hollywood and it firmly entrenched my belief in ghosts."

Lizzie opened the door and brought in the pie. Holding it proudly like she had baked it herself, but he could tell it was from Fleishem's bakery, which was a popular new bakery in the more artsy section of Portland.

"What kind is it?" he asked.

"It's pumpkin," Hazel said. "I know it's spring, but it's been so chilly and drizzly lately, I felt pumpkin pie was appropriate. This weather today certainly called for a good, old-fashioned pumpkin pie with whipped cream on top. Something to warm your belly."

"I agree," Caleb said appreciatively.

Lizzie grinned. "I love pumpkin pie."

Hazel beamed, her eyes twinkling. "It's my favorite too."

It warmed his heart to see his daughter so happy, and there was a part of him that this felt was right. The problem was, it couldn't last. He had no time to even think of romance right now. He had a teenage daughter, a job, and didn't have the emotional capacity to give more. Not to mention that whenever he'd mentioned Lizzie in the past, women weren't interested.

Which was fine by him. He didn't have time for them either.

Except now it didn't feel that fine.

There was also a part of him that was scared of letting someone in again.

He remembered the visceral pain of Jane's loss still.

He was terrified of that deep, gut-wrenching agony he'd felt the night he'd held his newborn daughter in his arms and learned that his wife was gone.

That pain he kept buried deep inside, to remind

him that he was never going to go through that again. He couldn't.

His heart wouldn't survive it.

"Lizzie, are you okay?" Hazel asked.

He glanced up to see that Lizzie looked a bit green around the gills.

"Lizzie?" He got up and touched her head. "You're feverish."

"I just feel a bit sick. I think I'll lie down for a bit."

"Can I get you anything?" Caleb asked.

"Maybe Hazel could help me?" Lizzie asked.

"Sure," Hazel said. She helped her up and they left the room.

He was confused.

Usually he was the one who took care of his daughter when she was sick. Why was she asking for Hazel?

Of course, the older Lizzie got the less she wanted him to help.

Hazel came back. "She's fine. Just a bit queasy."

"Queasy?" he asked.

Hazel's eyes widened. "Yes, well, stress, classes and you know how it is at this age."

"I do."

Although, he felt like she was holding something back.

Are you sure about that?

"Let's finish our dessert, shall we?"

"That would be great," Hazel said promptly.

They ate their pumpkin pie and talked about nothing in particular. After the pie was finished, Caleb walked Hazel to the door.

She pulled on her sensible boots over the rainbow toe socks.

"Thank you for having me over for dinner. Lizzie is a wonderful cook."

Caleb smiled. "Thank you for coming. You made her night. Sorry she got sick."

"She's a lovely young woman. Seriously, any time she needs anything, just tell me. I know we haven't exactly gotten along before…"

He winced. "That is my fault. I do apologize. I could've explained myself better at the tribunal."

"You're not the only one at fault. I was exceptionally mad that day."

He smiled gently. "You certainly were."

That blush tinged her cheeks again. "Well, I'm sorry too."

"I appreciate that. I'm glad we cleared the air."

Hazel nodded. There was a small dimple in her right cheek. One that he wanted to kiss. The impulse caught him off guard, so he took a step back to disconnect. He couldn't let this go too far. Even if his instincts were telling him that he should kiss her, pull her into an embrace. He couldn't do that.

She was a professional colleague.

That's all they could be. That's what he wanted. *Isn't it?*

"Well, good night," he said abruptly, not sure what to do.

"Good night, Caleb." She opened the door and headed out into the drizzly spring night. He watched her from the door as she made her way to her car. His head was a jumbled mess as she drove away.

There was a part of him that so wanted more.

Only she wasn't his for the taking.

CHAPTER FOUR

A FEW DAYS had passed since Hazel had been over to his place for dinner, and Caleb couldn't stop thinking about her. And it wasn't just the dinner; it was her collaboration on Mrs. Jameson's vaginal birth after caesarean case.

As head of obstetrics, his work was fairly solitary, other than teaching his residents or conferring with anesthesiology, nurses and the chief of staff.

It was rare to have such a collaboration with a professional colleague.

It was nice.

He stared out at the birthing center across the road.

There was a knock at the door.

"Come."

Victor Anderson stuck his head in. "Hey, how are you doing today?"

Caleb glanced over his shoulder and then turned to face him. "Good. And you?"

"Very good, surprisingly, considering I just had a meeting with the board of directors." Victor winced and Caleb chuckled as his colleague came into the office and sat down.

"So what did the new chairman have to say this time?" Caleb asked.

"Timothy is still so convinced that the Women's

Health Center across the road will be detrimental to St. Raymond's finances."

"Why is he so concerned about St. Raymond's bottom line? According to the last fiscal statement the board passed around to staff heads, we're not hurting for money. We both know the Women's Health Center will be mutually beneficial. Why can't he see that too?" Caleb asked.

Victor shrugged. "Who knows? It's quite frustrating. If I had my way, there would be no more endless meetings about it. I wish Timothy Russell would just accept that the Women's Health Center is going to stay, and there's nothing to be done about it. It's time to move on to the more pressing needs of the hospital. Those midwives aren't villains, they're just doing their jobs. Like we need to be doing ours."

Caleb sighed. "It seems to me that our time or rather the board of directors' time could be used in a much better way."

Victor tapped his nose. "But you didn't hear it from me."

"Maybe I should go to speak with them."

Victor raised his eyebrows. "You want to talk to the board? To Timothy? You two don't exactly see eye to eye."

"Sure. There's a huge benefit to working with the midwives. They can send over surgical patients to us. It's a win-win."

"You know that and I know that," Victor said, agreeing.

"I'm currently utilizing Hazel Rees's knowledge on Mrs. Jameson, who Timothy is very eager for us to help. Well, for me to help."

"That's great! Just don't mention it to Timothy that Hazel is involved."

"What do you mean?" Caleb asked, confused. "Timothy already knows Hazel is involved."

Victor groaned. "Oh, no. He'll definitely try to do something about that."

"Are you serious, Victor? You mean he would try to stop the collaboration even though he knows it's what the patient wishes?"

Victor sighed. "Yes."

"That's ridiculous."

Victor nodded. "Agreed. I'm still going to try to get the board to agree that working with the birthing center is the best thing for everyone involved, but with Timothy Russell at the helm, it'll be hard."

"Should I present them with some more facts?" Caleb asked hotly. "Since they got me to present so many at that tribunal."

Victor grinned. "If you'd like to, you can tell them the senior staff will put up a united front to support the birthing center."

"That could work."

Victor stood up. "It sounds like a plan."

"Is that all you wanted to discuss?" Caleb asked.

"Yes." Victor winked. "Just making my rounds

and I peeked in and saw you staring out your window in quiet contemplation. Usually you're hard at work, head down at charting."

Caleb grinned. "Well, maybe it's time to stop and smell the roses."

He had been so distracted lately. All he could think about was Hazel. Her smile, her laughter, that dimple in her cheek. It was more than a bit consuming. It had been a while since he'd felt this way about someone, not since Jane. No other women had held him in this kind of thrall in a very long time.

It had also been forever since he'd let someone take up this much space in his brain.

Victor left his office with a wave as he shut the door. Caleb was left feeling incredibly frustrated that Timothy Russell didn't see the value of the birthing center.

What was happening to St. Raymond's? It used to be such a great place to work. He'd always loved coming here every day, but lately it was all becoming too much like a big corporation.

It was more about the money than the medicine.

The old board of directors would have been all for a collaboration. The new chairman would ruin this hospital's reputation if he wasn't careful.

"Hey, Dad!"

Caleb turned to see Lizzie come in. She still looked a little pale, and he was worried about her.

"How are you feeling?" he asked.

"Fine. It was just a bit of a stomach bug. Stress about midterms." Lizzie set her bag down.

He wasn't sure that was completely it. There was something else going on, but she was being tight-lipped.

Maybe she broke up with Derek?

He knew he had to tread lightly with her private life, or he'd get pushback.

Lizzie could be as stubborn as he was.

"What're you doing here?" Caleb asked.

"Can't I come see my dad?" she retorted.

He chuckled. "Of course."

"Good." She worried on her bottom lip. "There's something I need to talk to you about."

"About midwifery? It's okay if you want to study that. I'd prefer it if you went to medical school so you could follow in my footsteps," he teased.

Although, he didn't care what she did for a career, as long as she was happy and could take care of herself.

Lizzie's eyes were wide. "Right."

"Was that it?" he asked.

"Yes. That was it."

"If you're going to learn midwifery then Hazel is one of the best."

"She's great," Lizzie agreed.

He had a feeling that there was more she wanted to talk about, but then his pager went off.

"One of your patients?" Lizzie asked.

"Yes. She's been brought in and I have to check on her."

"Go." Lizzie got up and kissed him on the cheek. "I'll see you later."

Caleb left and headed down to the labor and delivery floor. He was so distracted today. He had to get his head on straight.

He had to concentrate.

Caleb hated this loss of control over his own thoughts. Being in control was how he'd managed his life for the last eighteen years.

It's how he'd raised his daughter, made his way through medical school and it would be how he got over his infatuation with Hazel.

"What in the world are you reading?"

Hazel startled with a slight jump and looked up to see Bria hovering in the doorway of her office. She didn't even hear her come in. Hazel had been so engrossed in reading about the Black Dahlia murders, she had tuned out the world.

It had been a few days since her dinner with Caleb and Lizzie.

And all she could think about was how much she missed them. How nice it was to have dinner with a family again. Her family was scattered all over, and it had been some time since she'd got together with her parents and siblings.

It was lovely to have that feeling of belonging. She had Bria, but both of them had been so busy trying to get the center up and running that when they'd each got to their respective homes, they'd simply crashed. Hazel's whole life had been this center, and her dinner at Caleb's home with Lizzie suddenly had her longing for something more.

Something she wanted so much, but she'd been burned before.

Her heart was still on lockdown because Mark had crushed her so completely. It was just better to be alone and focus on her career.

And to get her mind off Caleb, she had purchased a book about the old Hollywood murders. She hadn't heard the door open, and now her heart was racing a mile a minute! She set the book down, trying to regain her composure.

Bria cocked her head and looked at the cover. "What in the world is this about? Black Dahlia?"

"An old Hollywood murder that Caleb was talking about. I thought I would read up on it."

Bria smiled knowingly and cocked an eyebrow. "Caleb?"

Hazel's cheeks heated. "Dr. Norris... I mean."

Bria chuckled. "No, I don't think that you do. I think you meant Caleb. You went to his place for dinner, didn't you? How did that go?"

Wonderful.

Marvellous.

It felt like home.

"It was good," Hazel said quickly. "He grew up

with the Hollywood elite. His mother was a film star and his father a director."

Bria's eyes widened. "Are you serious?"

"Apparently his mother was in a Bond movie."

"That's wild! He doesn't seem like the type."

"Oh?" Hazel asked, but then she had thought the same thing too.

"Aren't all native Californians supposed to be laid-back?"

Hazel chuckled. "That's a stereotype. Being a military child, or brat, I would also like to sweep away textbook stereotypes."

"And he recommended you read about these Hollywood murders?" Bria asked, glancing at the cover of the book again.

"He did."

"Maybe he's a serial killer?"

It was a joke, but Hazel just shook her head and puffed out a breath. "What is it that you need?"

Bria nodded and held out a file. "New patient. She's coming in. I'm swamped, and Joan said you weren't answering your texts."

Hazel glanced at her phone and cursed under her breath. "It's on silent."

Bria handed her the file. "The patient will be here in ten minutes. Look sharp. Read on your own time and all that nonsense."

Hazel laughed. "Right. Thanks."

Bria nodded and left.

Hazel texted Joan to let her know when the patient came in. She glanced down at the book and sighed. It had been a long time since she had escaped into a book or done anything beyond work, eat, or sleep.

She was feeling slightly burned out lately. Getting their center off the ground had left her with very little time to relax, but that was the casualty of running your own business. She took another deep breath and opened the patient's file from their general practitioner. It was all standard stuff letting her know that the patient was pregnant.

This was her first pregnancy.

And it looked very textbook.

Hazel set down the file and then began to tidy up her desk.

Joan called her.

"Hi," Hazel answered.

"Your next patient, Sandra Patterson, is here," Joan said.

"Send her in." Hazel hung up and waited to greet the patient.

She walked into the room with her husband, and the first thing that Hazel noticed was that the woman was considerably larger than she should be for fourteen weeks. She shouldn't even be showing that much, especially for a first pregnancy.

Instantly she saw a red flag.

"Sandra, it's a pleasure to meet you. I'm Hazel."

Sandra smiled. "The pleasure is all mine. This is my husband, Dan."

Hazel shook Dan's hand.

Dan looked a bit frazzled, a bit stunned, which wasn't uncommon for a first pregnancy, but he was also smiling, so he seemed to be happy to be here.

"Have a seat," Hazel said, motioning to the chairs.

Her mind was already going a mile a minute as she looked at Sandra, and her instinct was telling her there were multiple fetuses. She'd seen it once before, a case of quadruplets when she was in her nursing training, before she decided to completely focus on midwifery.

High-order pregnancies were always difficult.

Sandra and Dan sat down, and Hazel shut the door to her office.

"Congratulations on your pregnancy," Hazel said brightly.

"Thank you!" Sandra was beaming, but poor Dan still looked a little shocked.

"I was told that I didn't really have to see a midwife straightaway," Sandra said.

"No, not right away," Hazel agreed.

"My cycle is so unpredictable," Sandra said.

"I've had a glance at your file. You're about fourteen weeks along?"

Sandra nodded. "I was prepping to do in vitro fertilization. We had been trying for some time, but again I'm not totally sure. My cycle was so sporadic."

"Well, we can do a dating ultrasound to confirm.

Were you taking any medication for egg production?" Hazel asked, another red flag rising to attention that this was multiple gestation.

"Yes, we were getting ready to harvest, but then I noticed my temperature was right and we just got pregnant." Sandra smiled at Dan and he returned that loving smile, squeezing her hand.

"Have you had an ultrasound?" Hazel asked.

Sandra shook her head. "No. When my doctor confirmed my pregnancy, I weighed my options. I really wanted to see a midwife first. Which is why I'm here. It takes me some time to think."

Hazel smiled as she inputted the information into Sandra's chart.

"That's not a problem, but given that you were taking medication to start an egg harvest, there is a good chance that you could be carrying multiples."

Dan's face went paler. "Multiples?"

"We'll do an ultrasound and see, shall we?" Hazel suggested. "That way we can give you a good date estimate."

Sandra nodded. "Okay."

"Climb up on the exam table, and I'll pull out my handy-dandy portable ultrasound."

Sandra nodded again. "If I have more than one, will I still be able to deliver here? I really don't want to go to the hospital. It's not in my birth plan."

"I'll lay it out straight. We can for sure safely deliver twins here. We've done that before. Anything above two, though, I'm going to bring in an obstetrician to consult. You can absolutely continue to have your care here as long as you and the babies stay healthy, but there are risks for anything over two. Ninety percent of births over two are delivered via caesarean section, but there are some small percentages that can still deliver vaginally. It's not hopeless."

"Okay." Sandra eased onto the exam table and lay down.

Dan stood next to her. "I just want Sandra to be healthy."

"Of course," Hazel said, smiling.

Hazel got everything ready to do the ultrasound. She hadn't meant to terrify the new parents, her new patients, but the fact was they had to be made aware of the possibilities. If they were in the process of upping Sandra's egg production and it wasn't a controlled procedure, there was a huge likelihood of twins or even triplets.

Sandra lifted her shirt and Hazel did measurements of her belly. Her patient was definitely measuring large for fourteen weeks, which was confirming her suspicions.

"Okay, this jelly is a bit cold." She squirted the jelly on Sandra's lower abdomen and flicked on her ultrasound.

It didn't take long for Hazel to find the uterus and her hunch was correct, but as she counted the egg sacks, the little flickering of heartbeats, her hope for a safe delivery of twins was quickly dashed. She counted five.

Five viable heartbeats.

Five little lives.

"Well…" And Hazel was at a loss for words. "How long have you two been trying?"

"A long time," Dan said. "We always hoped for a large family, but as the years went on that kind of became a pipe dream."

"You're going to get your wish." Hazel moved the monitor. "There are your babies. Five of them in fact."

"Five!" Sandra gasped, tears welling in her eyes. "Five! Like as in quints?"

"Quints occurring naturally are extremely rare," Hazel remarked. "And though you were taking medication to increase your harvest, this is still pretty momentous news. It also means I would definitely like to have an obstetrician brought in. With a multiple pregnancy like this, we're looking at a preterm birth, possible gestational diabetes…so this is the safest thing for you and your babies."

Dan looked down at Sandra, smiling. "Okay, but we don't know any good obstetricians. We're new to Portland."

"I happen to know an excellent one, who is just across the street." Hazel saved a picture of the babies and wiped off the jelly. She handed Sandra the printed picture. "If you two wouldn't mind waiting here, I'll give him a call now and see if he can come over to meet you."

Sandra and Dan nodded. Not saying much as they stared in wonder at the sonogram.

It warmed her heart.

High-order pregnancies were dangerous, but she could see the longing etched in Sandra's and Dan's faces. They were happy. Terrified, but happy with their outcome.

Hazel slipped out of her office and pulled out her phone.

She typed in Caleb's office number.

This was too important for a text or even an email.

This warranted a call.

"Dr. Norris speaking," he said stiffly.

"Caleb, it's Hazel."

"Hazel?" he asked, confused. "I haven't input your number, but it came up as a private caller."

"Yeah, I have it set that way. Sorry. Anyways, you remember how you said you'd be willing to consult with me?"

"I do," he said cautiously.

"I have a need for one. Big time."

"What is it? You sound a bit shaken."

"It's quints. Conceived naturally…for the most part. They're here now, and I could really use your help with this one."

There was a slight pause. "I'll be there in twenty minutes."

She could hear the excitement in his voice. She couldn't blame him. This was thrilling. She hadn't seen quints since her days of training, and even then she'd just observed. She wasn't involved in the delivery.

High-order births, especially ones like this, were just so rare. This would be an exciting case. A challenging case.

Hazel hung up and then took another deep breath. She headed over to Joan at the reception desk.

"Hazel?" Joan asked. "You look like you've seen a ghost."

"Not quite. Dr. Norris is coming in. Please show him to my office right away when he gets here."

Joan nodded. "Of course."

Hazel headed back to her office.

When she had asked Caleb to work with her, she thought it would be once in a while, or not very often, but fate had apparently found a way to bring them together yet again.

First Mrs. Jameson's VBAC, Lizzie's pregnancy and now the quints.

It looked like for the next several months she and Caleb would be working very closely together. So much for putting distance between them.

Thanks, karma.

Caleb shook Dan Patterson's hand as he and Sandra left. The Pattersons had made it clear that they wanted to keep coming to the center to have their checkups, and Caleb didn't see a problem with that as long as the babies were small.

He ordered a bunch of tests.

Including monitoring Sandra for gestational diabetes, more often than he would with a singleton pregnancy.

He still couldn't quite believe that it was quints.

Although Sandra had taken medication to aid her with in vitro fertilization, she had still conceived the babies naturally and he found that fascinating. It was rare that he came across that. Usually the high-order births that came through St. Raymond's were because of IVF.

He was really glad that Hazel had asked him to consult on this case.

He knew she was a nurse practitioner and a midwife, but cases like this needed a bit more help. And he was only too glad to be involved.

"Thank you for coming over so quickly and for letting my patients continue their primary care here," Hazel said.

"You mean *our* patients. I'm glad to help, but there are so many complications we have to watch for, and when she gets to a certain point then I'm going to want her on bedrest."

"At the hospital?" Hazel asked.

"No, not necessarily. I mean the board of directors, I'm sure, would love me to assign her to months of hospital bed rest and rack up her medical bills."

"Of course. It's all about the money," Hazel groused.

"Indeed, but if she's well and the babies are fine, then I don't see why she can't stay at home for the time being. Eventually, we'll have to monitor her frequently the further along she gets. It's a huge adjustment and shock."

"Well, it doesn't matter how many babies are in there. I still see a lot of fathers with that deer in the headlights look on their face," Hazel said lightly.

"Agreed. I had a similar expression when my late wife told me the news."

They shared a smile.

"I can only imagine," Hazel said. "You must've been like…what, a young man when your late wife had Lizzie?"

"A lot younger indeed. I'm forty now."

"That's still very young to have a grown daughter!"

He smiled. "Perhaps."

And he thought back to that moment Jane had told him she was pregnant. He had been so surprised. A child that early hadn't been a part of his and Jane's plans, but the shock had been momentary, because then he'd felt an unending amount of joy when they'd learned they were going to be parents. He'd always wanted to be a father.

He wasn't always the most demonstrative when it came to his feelings, but he still felt those moments very deeply. It was just hard to feel anything when he'd had to keep it all together just to get through medical school and take care of Lizzie.

His little girl had never wanted for love, but that was all he could give for so many years as he'd chipped away at his enormous student debts.

Being wracked with pain and yet having a beautiful piece of yourself and your wife to love and protect. It had been such a fine line to walk for so many years, being a loving supportive father on the outside, maintaining a professional demeanor at school and work, but being a raw, broken mess inside when you were alone.

"I can only imagine," Hazel said, breaking through his thoughts. "Still, I'll need your expertise. At first, Sandra was quite adamant about her birth plan."

"Her birth plan will have to change," Caleb said bluntly.

"That's a bit harsh," Hazel responded.

"I've had run-ins with very controlling patients."

'That's quite the judgment of people you've only just met!"

"I'm just generalizing," Caleb said defensively.

"Well, a mother's birth plans are important."

"They are important, I agree, but they also need to be fluid. You can't predict every detail. Things happen during labor and delivery you can't control." He knew firsthand about those changes. It hadn't ever imagined he'd end up being a single father and a widower.

"I think it's something practical parents can do to ease stress, and what's wrong with that?" Hazel asked hotly.

"Look, I don't want to argue. I get why birth plans are important for a woman. It's their body and it's their right to dictate what they need, but I'm just pointing out that most times those birth plans are just that. A plan. An ideal that is meant to ease anxiety. Nature has its own agenda sometimes. I've rushed countless women into surgery who were adamant right up until the spinal epidural froze that they weren't going to cop out the easy way and have a C-section."

Hazel frowned. "A C-section is not a cop-out, nor is it easy. I see patients all the time who are post C-section and are working with adhesions and scar collapse, prolapse issues…just the same as someone who gave birth vaginally."

Caleb nodded. "Exactly, but misinformation and internet research can be misleading. People make ill-informed choices when they do their own medical research. Dr. Internet Search Engine is the worst kind of quackery."

Hazel relaxed as she chuckled. "Quackery?"

He grinned. "Exactly."

"It must be that undergraduate English literature coming out in you. You talk like a disgruntled hero from a Jane Austen novel."

"Do I?" He smiled at her. Her mention of literature had him remembering their dinner again; he'd been thinking about her a lot since that night. In fact, he couldn't get her out of his head, and that was a bit worrisome.

What was it about her that attracted him so? He never normally had this kind of preoccupation with a woman.

But Lizzie is an adult now. She doesn't need you now as much. You're free to pursue happiness.

And maybe that was it, but honestly he didn't know if it was the whole story. Perhaps it was simply Hazel.

Instead, he'd thrown himself into his work to try and not think about her. It had been working until she called him today, but he was still glad that she did. Quints were something special, and he was more than happy to be a part of the patient's care.

And it also would be interesting to see how working more closely with Hazel would be.

When they'd finally opened the clinic here, he'd done his research on her. He wanted to know who he could be potentially working with. So he'd learned what he could about the midwives, in particular Hazel. He knew where Hazel did her training and what papers she had written. She was impressive, and he was looking forward to working with her closely.

Truth be told, he was growing seriously tired of hospital politics.

And he was becoming more envious of her freedom to open her own practice. There was a part of him that wished he could leave Portland behind, open up his own practice somewhere up north… like in Alaska. Alaska had always been a secret dream of his since reading books set there when he was a child.

It was so different from his lonely life in Los Angeles and growing up as a Hollywood child.

Alaska made him think of peace, quiet and adventure.

Only, he couldn't do that to Lizzie.

His daughter needed security, and security meant him keeping a stable job. Opening up his own practice meant he'd be wholly financially responsible for its continued success. Caleb wasn't sure he could invest in himself and take that risk when Lizzie still needed him.

So he was stuck for now. At least until Lizzie was finished with school and was independent with her own life and that was fine.

Everything was fine.

Is it?

"You do. A bit," Hazel answered, interrupting his train of thought. "Except for the American accent. It's not quite as dignified as Mr. Darcy or anything."

"Thanks," he replied sardonically, deciding a change of subject was in order. "I'm glad your center will be able to handle the tests I need."

"We can't do an amniocentesis here. Not yet."

"We can handle that at St. Raymond's," Caleb answered. "It's a delicate procedure when it's a high-order pregnancy. We want to draw out the fluid, but not hurt a fetus. And then there's trying to figure out whether it was one egg that split and if there's different embryonic sacs."

"I remember seeing one set of quints, but it was from IVF, so they were different sacs. It's not too early to determine gender. If they were all the same gender, then we could probably deduce that they were from the same egg," Hazel said. "Like that case in Canada in the thirties...the quints they put on display because they were the first to live."

"Yes. They were all identical."

"I'll say it again, I am glad that you're willing to help me. I have other patients, and I'm a little out of my depth here. It's a lot of babies, potentially."

"Potentially?" he teased. "I think it's a fact."

"Of course. I don't know why I jumped to the idea that they might not all make it."

"It's a sobering thought, but with the right health care and with us working together, I think her babies have a great shot."

"All five of them," Hazel said brightly.

He smiled. "Indeed."

It was going to be a very high-risk pregnancy, but Caleb had this instinctual, gut feeling that working with Hazel would make things so much easier for them all. That this was the best course of treatment for Sandra Patterson and her babies.

"I think we'll make a good team."

"I do too."

They gazed at each other for a moment. His pulse was thundering between his ears. A pink blush tinged her cheeks, and it took all his will-power not to reach out and let his fingers brush across her skin.

He wanted to feel her softness.

Hazel looked at her phone. "Oh, I have to run! One of my patients is in labor and they're outside the city."

"Can I help?" he asked. "I have the afternoon off, and Lizzie is studying late tonight at her boy-friend's."

"You say that so disparagingly," she teased.

Caleb grunted. "Derek is an okay person. So can I help you?"

"I think I'll be fine, but thank you," she said quickly.

Caleb was slightly disappointed, but he couldn't blame her. This was her work. Would he really want her in the operating room with him while he was doing a surgical procedure?

Yes.

But he pushed that niggly little voice away.

"At least let me walk you to your car and help carry something?"

Hazel was grabbing the prepacked birthing kits.

"Okay. If you can grab that other duffel bag, you can help me lug it to my car so I can get out of here. It's a two-hour drive."

Caleb picked it up and followed Hazel out of her office and the building to her car. She opened the trunk, and they heaved everything in.

"Thanks again," she said, quickly shutting her trunk. "I'll call you later and we can talk further about Sandra Patterson."

"Sounds good."

Hazel smiled at him quickly and climbed in the car. He took a step back as she turned the ignition. Nothing happened. There was a small sputter of the engine, but it didn't turn over. She tried again, but had the same result.

She rolled down her window, wincing. "Can I ask another favor?"

"You need a lift to your patient's?" he asked.

She nodded. "If you don't mind."

"Not at all. Stay put. I'll be back in a few minutes with my car."

"Thanks." She leaned her head against her steering wheel and banged it gently a few times in frustration.

He couldn't blame her.

Normally, he'd be swamped, but today he was not on rotation for the delivery room and he had no patients to see. It was a day he usually dedicated to dictation, reports and research. It would be nice to get out of the office for a few hours and take Hazel to attend a birth. With Lizzie at Derek's, there was nothing waiting for him at home.

Except loneliness.

Even if he was used to it, he was glad for the excuse to have some company.

CHAPTER FIVE

HAZEL WAS VERY THANKFUL, but still shocked that she was sitting next to Caleb as they sped their way through curvy mountain roads toward her patient's house. Of all the days for her car to break down, it had to be today.

Her patient was no stranger to home births.

This was her seventh child born at home.

Hazel was more worried that she wasn't going to make it in time.

The roads were a bit slick from drizzle, and it was midafternoon. School buses were making their runs, and the trip became longer and longer. And the more time that went by, the more Hazel was worried that she would be too late and that she would've wasted Caleb's time driving out here.

It's not a waste of time. You're checking on your patient.

They hadn't said much as they raced out of the city to her patient's rural address, but it wasn't an awkward silence. It felt like it was normal. Like they had done this many times before, and Hazel couldn't help but wonder what had shifted in the last week.

For the last few months, he had been such a thorn in her side.

A sexy, broody thorn, but a thorn nonetheless.

Now it was as though they were friends or something.

It was weird, but also kind of nice.

She had Bria, but no one else thanks to her family being spread so far and wide.

And she didn't realize how lonely she had become. Of course, part of that was her own doing. She pushed people away, in particular men. It was safer for her heart. Especially after what Mark did to her.

She'd been destroyed after catching him in the act with Melody. It was so dehumanizing. It had broken her trust, and it was hard to let go of that pain. It was almost impossible to think about opening her heart again.

It was much easier to keep people out. Except for Bria. She still didn't quite know how her friend had managed that, but she was glad for it. The one thing she was certain of was that Bria wouldn't ever hurt her.

The wall she had erected around herself was for her own good, and she had to remember that. Even if there was a part of her that was telling her she was settled in Portland and it was okay to let people in now.

"You know," she said, finally breaking through the silence, "I really do appreciate the lift here. I could've called a cab. I'm sorry for burdening you."

She didn't know what had made her ask him for a ride, but she was glad she did as they followed the

Columbia River before turning south to go around Mount Hood National Park.

"You're not burdening me. Not at all. I told you that I was able to help you out. It's a nice distraction, this drive. It's a beautiful rainy spring day. Not a fan of the unseasonable cold though."

"I just hope we get there in time."

"You said this is her seventh child?" Caleb asked.

"Yep."

His eyebrows raised. "I think I'll go a wee bit faster."

She chuckled. "Don't get a ticket, but I'm very glad your GPS has the ability to provide alternate routes to bypass traffic and accidents."

The usual highway that she would take from Portland down past Warm Springs was backed up with a tractor trailer that had rolled over on the interstate.

Caleb had got the information and altered his course before the rest of the traffic was detoured the same way. Following the Columbia River took a little bit more time, but it was definitely better than sitting in a traffic jam and probably missing the birth.

As an added bonus, this was the more scenic route as far as Hazel was concerned. With Caleb driving it gave her a chance to sit back and prepare for her patient's birth.

"Is your patient fairly healthy? What I mean is, do her deliveries usually go smoothly? Do the infants fare well?" Caleb asked. "Should I call an ambulance on the off chance there's a problem?"

"No, she does fairly well. She's a pro and her babies are strong. We haven't had to call an ambulance yet. If we did, it would have to be an air ambulance as they live a little off the grid and just outside of Warm Springs."

He raised his eyebrows. "I really hope you make it on time. I almost wonder if they really need you."

"I do feel like an ornament sometimes with her," Hazel acknowledged. "But they like to have me there, and I don't blame them. You just never know what could happen."

"That is true," he said quietly, and she couldn't help but wonder if he was thinking of his late wife again. "I wish we knew how she was doing. I'm getting a bit anxious as well."

"I know. I've been getting texts from her husband and she's still laboring. Even if she does give birth before I get there, I can still do an assessment of the baby and make sure mother and baby are both okay."

"Seven kids," Caleb murmured. "I had a hard time raising one."

Hazel chuckled. "At least it's not seven all at once!"

"I've seen that once," he said sadly. "Almost lost the mother, and two of the babies were born with difficulties. One did not survive and..." He didn't continue his thought, but trailed off.

"What?" she asked gently. Although, she knew. It was the worst part of the job, when there was nothing to be done and a life was lost.

"I was only a student, but I remember the hospital bill that family faced. It still haunts me."

"Yet you work for a hospital that does similar things. Charges astronomical amounts."

"I needed to provide for my child," he said stiffly. "It doesn't mean I always like it. I don't set the fees. The board of directors does that."

He didn't need to say more. Hazel was quite familiar with the board of directors and their greedy policies at St. Raymond's.

"Do you do a lot of pro bono work?"

"I try to," he said. "Not as much as I would like."

Her heart softened. When she'd first met Caleb, she had painted a completely different picture of him. This was a different side to the man, one that she could relate to. She also wanted to help others. She'd grown up in a large family, and medical expenses could be tricky.

She'd seen families struggle.

Health care should be more affordable. That had always been her stand.

Not that it was a particularly popular opinion always, but she was glad to see that Caleb was sympathetic.

She tried to help where she could too.

She was glad that her first impression of him was incorrect.

He was a lot better than she thought he was. More honorable, and they had a lot more in common than she thought they did.

Don't get too attached, that persistent little voice reminded her. It warned her of the last time she'd let herself get too involved with a man she'd thought she was on the same wavelength with and how much that betrayal had hurt.

She was never going to risk her heart again.

Friends. Yes.

Lovers. No.

The thought of Caleb as her lover immediately made her blood heat and she shifted in her seat, hoping he didn't notice a blush in her cheeks.

"So I started reading about the Black Dahlia and those murders in old Hollywood," she said, trying to change the subject.

"Did you?" he asked, intrigued.

"In fact, Bria caught me reading it. She was kind of horrified, but she doesn't get my fascination with history and true crime."

"I don't get your fascination with old Hollywood. I told you, I lived the aftermath. It's not all that glamourous. It was kind of a miserable childhood, if I'm honest. My mother on sets, my dad at constant parties trying to make connections."

"You said your mother was in a Bond movie. Which Bond?" she asked.

He chuckled. "It was a small part."

"Oh, come on, which one?"

Caleb cleared his throat and tried a very garbled Scottish accent that was terribly bad. "Guess."

"Really? That's exciting. He was so handsome. Even right up until the end, when he was older."

"Never understood why women were so entranced by him."

"Did you ever meet him?"

"No. Bond was before my time. My mom became pregnant shortly after that movie, and I was born."

"Maybe you're really his love child."

Caleb laughed. "Uh, no, I can assure you I am very much my father's son. Though, whenever I got mad at him I did fantasize that James Bond was indeed my father, and he was going to rescue me to take me on exciting adventures. I'm talking about the fictional version, by the way, the character from Ian Fleming's books. I was very much over Hollywood as a child."

"Still, it's kind of exciting. We were a transient family, being military and all."

"So where was the most exciting place you moved to?" he asked.

"Alaska. Nome, Alaska. Like far up there."

"See, and now I'm jealous of that."

She quirked an eyebrow. "You're jealous of me living in Alaska?"

"Completely. It was sort of a dream for a long time to move up there and open a practice, but my late wife didn't want to leave Portland and then

I had Lizzie and those dreams just became that. Dreams."

"I understand that. Although, I have to admit I'm living my dream at the moment."

"Oh?" he asked.

"It was always my dream to open a midwife clinic with Bria. I love being a midwife and taking care of women in all stages of health. There were some places where I've lived and worked where women's health wasn't freely discussed, and I was a bit sad to learn of places where a woman didn't have autonomy over her own body. I guess I wanted to change that. It took a long time. There were things I had to give up to make it happen."

What she didn't tell him was that she'd given up on the idea of finding Mr. Right after Mark. It was hard to believe in love when your heart was broken, though there was a part she kept locked away that still secretly hoped for a family of her own.

One small ember of hope left burning that she would find love.

That she could heal. But the logical part of her just had a hard time trusting again. She had sort of settled on the idea that she would be alone for the rest of her life, but that was okay with her.

Is it?

She ignored that thought again.

"I'm glad that you're living your dream," he said. They shared a brief glance, and she could see the sincerity in his eyes.

It made her stomach do a flip.

Silence fell between them again as they drove through the town of Warm Springs. It was down in the foothills of Mount Hood, which rose in their rearview mirror. They drove for another thirty minutes until the GPS told Caleb to take a sharp right and then a left down a bumpy, gravel track through the woods.

At the end of the long tract, Hazel could see the little log cabin that was nestled into the woods. Her patient Clarissa and her husband, Matt, had chosen to live like old-time homesteaders. The land had been in Matt's family for a long time.

They had modern conveniences, but those conveniences were run off solar power, water power and wind.

Matt was waiting outside as Caleb parked the car. Pacing more like it, holding his phone.

Matt looked worried, which made Hazel's stomach do another flip, this time in anxiety. Matt was never the one to be worried. Especially when this was Clarissa's seventh child. Hazel had delivered the last two, and she'd got to know the couple quite well.

So seeing Matt outside pacing, his face creased with worry, made her stomach knot in apprehension.

Hazel got out of the car and grabbed her first duffel.

Matt ran down the stairs from the front porch,

out into the rain. "You're a sight for sore eyes, Hazel. I was getting so worried."

"Sorry. Car troubles and then that accident on the interstate. I had to take a different route. This is Dr. Norris from St. Raymond's. He's accompanying me today. He was my ride."

Matt nodded, barely glancing at Caleb. "This labor is taking too long. None of the others have ever been like this. She's in a lot more pain than usual."

She began to mentally list in her head everything she had been worried about. All the reasons why this labor wasn't progressing.

Hazel nodded. "Let's go."

Caleb carried the other duffel bag full of her equipment as Matt gave her the full rundown about how labor had been going.

Or rather, how it hadn't, in this case.

The house was unusually quiet, but Matt explained that the kids were with his parents in town, so Clarissa could focus. Hazel was glad that the other kids were gone, because she needed the space to think.

When she walked into the bedroom, Clarissa was on all fours, panting and sweating. Hazel could see the pain etched on her face. More pain than was usual for her.

"Clarissa, tell me what's going on," Hazel asked as she opened her duffel bag and started to get the items out of her birthing kit. Clarissa was quite in tune with her body, and Hazel knew she would be able to articulate what wasn't right.

"It's taking too long. Feels. Stuck." Clarissa groaned. "This position felt better than lying down."

"You do what feels good," Hazel said encouragingly.

Hazel sanitized her hands and then pulled on gloves as Clarissa's glassy expression fell on Caleb.

"Who's that?" Clarissa asked.

"He's a doctor. A friend of mine. He's an OB/GYN, and he was working on an earlier case with me. My car broke down," Hazel said as she continued prepping.

Clarissa laughed weakly. "Your car is in bad shape. Told you that before."

Hazel grinned. "I know."

"What do you need me to do?" Caleb asked, setting down the other bag.

"Pull out the equipment and sanitize. I think the baby might have its shoulder stuck."

"Shoulder dystocia?" Caleb nodded. "She's had six natural births before?"

Hazel nodded. "It'll take some maneuvering, but I don't think we'll have to cut her. Just in case, though…"

Caleb nodded. "I'll prepare the instruments for an episiotomy."

"Thank you." Hazel made her way over to the bed. "It feels better this way? On all fours?"

Clarissa nodded, her gaze focusing as another

contraction tore through her. Hazel coached her through it.

"Good, Clarissa. Breathe, and I'm going to take a look if that's okay with you?"

Clarissa nodded. "Please."

Hazel knelt down. She could see the baby crowing with the contraction, but as the baby moved forward, it retracted, like a turtle.

Yep. She was pretty positive it was shoulder dystocia.

"Caleb, I'm going to need your help. Matt, I would like you to hold Clarissa's shoulders. I can't have her move." Hazel sat down behind her.

Caleb came over. "I have resuscitation equipment at the ready."

"Good. I don't think I need to do an episiotomy. If I can get her to deliver this way, there's going to be a little shift and we'll deliver the posterior shoulders first. I'll need your help keeping her steady, and I may need you to push on her abdomen."

"Of course." Caleb knelt down.

Hazel watched closely as the next contraction was coming. "Okay, Clarissa, I'm going to need you to push. As hard as you can."

Clarissa cried out. Hazel guided her hand to press on Clarissa's abdomen, while Caleb steadied her hips. The turtling effect stopped and the posterior shoulder appeared. There was a release and the baby began to slip through, no longer stuck.

"Push, Clarissa. Push!" Hazel urged.

Clarissa gave one final push, her body shaking as the baby was born into Hazel's hands. The baby didn't cry, and Clarissa was bleeding. Hazel quickly clamped the cord and Caleb took the small baby girl in his strong, steady hands.

"It's a girl," Hazel announced. "Matt, help me get her to lie down," she added, looking over her shoulders as Caleb took the baby over to the table, to where the portable oxygen tank she'd brought with her was kept.

"Why isn't she crying?" Clarissa whimpered.

"She was stuck, so Dr. Norris is tending to her. I'm going to see to you," Hazel said gently. Her pulse was thundering in her ears and her ears were pricked, listening for that cry of life. That first breath, but the room remained quiet.

Hazel kept her focus on making sure that Clarissa was stable.

Then she heard it.

The thin little wail through the room.

Hazel smiled and sighed internally. Matt and Clarissa cried out in relief.

Caleb was in awe of Hazel. She knew exactly what was wrong at almost first glance. She knew her patient so well and trusted her. For the first time, in a long time, since Lizzie was born really, he had felt absolutely the bystander during a birth.

It was clear that Clarissa was in very capable hands.

If Clarissa had walked into St. Raymond's and been in his care, he would've done the same thing. Although, there might be a surgeon or two who would've gone instantly to a caesarean section, but it was clear to him that it wasn't needed here.

He looked down at the tiny girl who had got stuck.

She was a little blue, but once he cleared her throat and nose with suction and gave her a bit of oxygen, she was improving. Her color was pinking up nicely.

Usually, when he delivered an infant that had a hard time breathing at first, the infant was whisked off by the attending pediatrician. His concern was the delivery. It was rare that he really got to be here and hold the new baby.

Hazel came over. "How is she?"

"Doing well. She just needed some help," Caleb said gently. "She's seven pounds three ounces. I took the liberty of measuring her. Her clavicle is broken, so they should get it checked by their pediatrician, but it's not uncommon for births like this. It'll heal on its own."

"She won't be in pain?" Clarissa asked.

"Should we give her pain meds?" Matt asked anxiously.

"No, she's too young. Just be mindful of the way you hold her," Hazel said.

She smiled as Caleb handed her the baby. Hazel took the little girl over to the happy parents, and he watched them. A bit jealous, like he always was when he saw first-time parents with their newborns.

He was happy for them, but it always brought him back to that moment.

The moment when he should've been the happiest he'd ever been and yet instead his world had shattered into a million pieces.

"Look at you. You're the most beautiful girl in the world. Your mommy is going to just love you."

He gently rocked his newborn daughter back and forth.

"Little Lizzy. It's what your mommy, Jane, wanted to call you. So you could be Lizzy and Jane, from Pride and Prejudice.*"*

He walked the hallway outside the delivery room. Jane went in for an emergency caesarean. Her spinal hadn't worked, and they'd to put her under. It wasn't uncommon. It happened to patients of his before, so he just waited.

It was when he glanced up at the clock and saw the time that passed that he began to worry. Only he couldn't freak out. He had a little life in his hands.

A little cherubic angel.

His daughter.

Still, watching the clock soon became an obsession for him.

And then a nurse ran by carrying blood.

His heart sank, because the nurse wouldn't look him in the eye.

His stomach knotted and he focused on the operating room doors. Waiting.

Time seemed to stand still.

Then his colleague came out. It was then that Caleb knew what happened. He held Lizzie closer.

"Tell me," Caleb said softly.

Though he already knew.

"I'm sorry, Caleb. We did everything we could. She bled so heavily, and then there was a pulmonary embolism. Her heart stopped. We brought in a cardiothoracic surgeon, but her heart... I'm so sorry."

Caleb sat down on the bench.

Numb.

Frozen.

Lizzie began to wail.

A wail that filled his heart with an unspoken scream of pain.

Caleb shook that memory away as he stared at the happy family now. That wasn't their story, and he was genuinely happy for them. Hazel was doting on the baby, and he couldn't help but smile at her.

There was just so much to like about her.

He hated that the board of directors was so against the midwife clinic.

The board of directors, in particular Timothy Russell, should work with Hazel and Bria's birthing center. It would be beneficial to all the pregnant women in the area. There was so much potential for a successful collaboration.

If only Timothy, the new and clueless chairman of the board, could see it. Caleb wished he and Hazel could be partners. Full on partners working on every case together.

Only, he worked in a hospital and she had her own business.

They couldn't be partners.

They could be friends, but that was it.

Even if there was a part of him that wanted more. In this moment, he wanted so much more and he was genuinely terrified of that. For so long he had been holding back. He'd had a child to raise, so much on his plate.

He hadn't thought he could love again, had believed that if he did try to open his heart he was somehow betraying Jane. The thing was, it was all just excuses, and he knew it, but he was still scared of what he was feeling. The need to move on and start anew was unknown.

Wanting more out of life was something he hadn't felt in a long, long time.

CHAPTER SIX

CALEB DIDN'T SAY MUCH.

All he could do was help Hazel clean up. The baby was doing well and Matt had made a call to their local doctor, who came out and checked on the baby. Once they were sure that Clarissa was well and everyone was stable, he carried the bags back out to his car while Hazel said her goodbyes.

He knew that Hazel was planning to come back out here to check on Clarissa and the baby. At the hospital, it usually depended on the shift rotation if he'd see his patients once after the birth, then six weeks after and then maybe not again.

Hazel had more of a chance to have a real relationship with her patients. He didn't really get that personal connection at St. Raymond's.

It was getting dark, and they still had a long drive back to Portland.

The rain was coming in harder.

He checked in with Lizzie, who told him she was still studying with Derek and then would be going to her friend's for the weekend. He hoped it was a friend and not Derek's. He knew that Lizzie was an adult, but he didn't want her to end up young, pregnant and still in school. That had been a challenge he hadn't enjoyed. Still, Caleb didn't really relish the idea of going back to an empty house.

It had never bothered him much before, but tonight he didn't want to be alone.

Hazel climbed into the car and they both waved at Matt, who had walked them out. Caleb didn't say much as he turned around in the drive and headed back down the bumpy track to the main road.

He didn't want this night with Hazel to end. He was enjoying his time with her. He liked working with her, and when they spent time together he forgot how lonely he was.

"You okay?" Hazel asked, breaking the awkward silence that had fallen between them.

"I'm fine. It was just…it's always a bit emotional watching new parents. You'd think I'd be used to it by now."

"I get it," she said wistfully.

"I'm sorry. I know I sound completely maudlin." He glanced over at her, sending her a smile. "I'll be okay though. Would you like to stop and get something to eat? It's well past dinnertime."

"Yes. I would love that, but it'll be my treat since you drove me out here and made dinner the last time."

"There's a small diner on the main interstate. It looks like a reasonable place. I've passed it before."

"Let's go there."

After a forty-minute drive from Matt and Clarissa's small homestead and back into the foothills of Mount Hood, they saw the neon lights through the dark and rain. The diner was sort of themed like a mountain lodge and was called Elkoholic, and there was a huge neon, animated sign of an elk looking extraordinarily happy with a stein of beer in its hoof.

It was tacky and kitschy, but it was warm, dry and provided food.

He just hoped it wasn't a dive.

"It's got great reviews, although the restaurant name is slightly dubious," Hazel said, holding up her phone.

"If it's got good reviews, then I'm slightly more relieved," Caleb said.

"Not into game meat?" she asked.

"It's how it's cooked and the cleanliness of the kitchen that's the concern."

"I wouldn't mind an elk steak or caribou. It's been some time since I've had either of those."

"Can't say that I've had caribou," he remarked. "What else have you eaten?"

"Let's see, deer, elk, caribou, moose and seal."

"Seal?" he asked, surprised.

"Nome, Alaska, remember? A friend of mine was Inupiat, and her mother let me try some seal oil and some of the seal."

"What did you think?"

"I wasn't overly keen, but it keeps you warm during a cold Alaska night."

"I'm sure."

He parked the car and they both made a mad dash through the rain to the entrance of the restaurant, just as the downpour was ending and the sun was coming out. Not that the sun would be up for much longer anyways. Inside was all wooden beams, hunting paraphernalia, canoes and other woodsmen and outdoors stuff.

It was like a lodge.

"Table for two?" the girl at the counter asked.

"Yes, please," Hazel said. "A booth would be great if you have one?"

"I do. Follow me," the girl said, smiling. She led them past happy patrons, lots of families to a back corner. There was a hidden booth that was covered in red flannel and dark wood. The table looked like it was a living-edge piece.

It was cozy and quiet, and he was thankful for the break to collect his thoughts.

The waitress placed two menus on the table. "I'll be back with some water and cornbread."

Caleb thanked her and slipped off his damp coat, sliding into the booth next to Hazel as she scooted to the far side of the table.

"This looks great! It sort of reminds me of a lodge my dad went to a lot in Nome. Only, it might've had something to do with moose or caribou."

"I've never seen a moose and you've eaten one," Caleb remarked, trying to change the subject from the recent birth and the feelings that had threatened to drown him afterward. Maybe if they talked about something else he wouldn't think about the day he'd lost Jane or about how much he liked being with Hazel.

Except for the fact he was with Hazel right now. Alone.

He glanced up and saw a stuffed elk hanging on the wall above her head. Its glassy eyes were staring at him, in what looked like horror.

Well, maybe they weren't totally alone.

"You're frowning. Actually, scowling is more like it."

He shook his head. "I was staring at your company there."

Hazel glanced over her shoulder and chuckled when she saw the elk head. "Oh, you know it's fake, right?"

"It's fake? How can you tell?"

"There's a tag that says it's from China. Also, it's felted. That's not real fur. It's close, but it's definitely not a real elk head."

"It's creepy anyway," he murmured, staring back down at the menu.

"Not a hunter?" she asked.

"Are you?" he retorted, cocking an eyebrow.

"No, but my dad was. Elk is not my favorite."

"What was your favorite then?"

"Are we really having a discussion about what my favorite kind of meat is?" she asked, her dark eyes twinkling.

He chuckled. "I suppose we are. I do have to

apologize for that. I'm not one for a lot of sparkling conversation."

"I don't know about that. I thought our conversation a couple of nights ago at your place was quite engaging. You're easy to talk to." A blush tinged her cheeks, and his heart began to beat a bit faster.

"You're easy to talk to as well."

The waitress came back and took their orders and then left again. He couldn't tear his eyes off Hazel's animated face. "You impressed me today."

"I seem to keep doing that, and I think it's quite unfair!"

"Oh?" he asked.

"I haven't had the chance yet to really see you in your element, but I suppose that your hospital board won't like me poking around too much."

"Probably not, but you know I would love to have you come and work with me being my on call consultant."

She cocked an eyebrow. "Are you serious?"

"You're a licensed medical professional. You're a midwife and I'm head of obstetrics. The board may not have the warmest attitude toward your health center, but they can't actually stop you from coming to the hospital. Besides, when Mrs. Patterson comes for a more extensive ultrasound, I would like you there. She is our patient, after all."

Hazel smiled, the little dimple that he found completely delectable showing up again. "I would like that."

"Then you can compliment me," he teased.

"Oh, so that's the game you're playing at then?" she joked.

"Well, you didn't want to discuss my previous topic about the various meats that you've tried and liked. Have you tried bear?"

Hazel started to laugh and she shook her head. "You are persistent, Mr. Hollywood."

Caleb wrinkled his nose. "That's the best you can do?"

She leaned across the table. "I tell you what. I'll tell you if I've had bear and you tell me about the time you stayed at the Black Dahlia murder house!"

"The supposed murder house," he corrected her. "Is it a deal?"

"Fine." He leaned back at crossed his arms. "What do you want to know?"

"Is it haunted? It's supposed to be haunted."

"If it is, I don't know. The only thing I remember about that house was that it was architecturally beautiful."

"Boring. Seriously."

"What do you want me to say? I was only ten at the time."

"At ten you were already appreciating architecture?" she asked with a smile.

"Not completely, but I remember thinking it looked cool. Is that good enough for you?" he asked.

"'Cool' I can believe. Especially for a ten-year-old."

"Now it's your turn," he said.

"Yes. I've had bear. I don't recommend it either."

"Was that so hard?"

The waitress came back with their drinks and their dinner on a large serving tray that she was balancing on one hand, quite impressively. All talk about consuming weird meat and the murder house that he went to when he was ten and growing up among the Hollywood glitterati dissipated, and instead they discussed the quints.

It was so easy to talk to her about medicine.

Jane hadn't been able to talk shop with him, but she had been a very good listener. It was kind of refreshing to talk about cases with Hazel, and for the first time in a long time he really enjoyed himself.

He completely lost track of time.

Instead of standing still, time sped up and soon the diner was shutting down and Hazel was stifling a yawn. They still had the best part of a two-hour drive to get back to Portland. Hazel paid the bill and he got a coffee to go.

It felt natural as they left the Elkoholic lodge and walked back to his car.

Only this time, when the silence came, it wasn't awkward. It was because Hazel had drifted off to sleep.

He glanced at her a few times, and he couldn't help but smile.

It felt so right with her here beside him, but he was afraid.

Afraid that if he did let her into his heart fully, she wouldn't want to reciprocate. If she rejected him, it would make working with her even more awkward. Why get involved with someone you often worked with? A middle-aged widower with a hefty amount of emotional baggage wasn't exactly appealing, at least that's what he thought.

Hazel certainly didn't appear to have that kind of baggage with her. She was young still, only late twenties, and unencumbered. He wasn't going to burden her with his past because he knew it would only drive her away in the end. His heart just couldn't take that kind of loss again.

Hazel hadn't realized that she'd drifted off until the car slowed down. She opened her eyes to see the lights of Portland in the distance. She touched her face gently, just to make sure that she wasn't drooling. She sometimes had the habit of doing that when she was very tired.

And today had been emotionally draining on so many levels.

She was pretty sure that her walls were still strongly in place. At least she liked to think they were. Except, when it came to Caleb, she could feel him edging around those barriers and it drove her crazy. Every time she saw him or spent time with him she always told herself that she was going to distance herself from him.

Then she didn't.

Caleb was a good man. What would he want with someone like her? A person who was not a particularly great judge of character. Someone who had been easily duped by a false love and made to look a fool. And if that wasn't enough, it was now clear to her why Caleb was still single. Because he'd never found anyone that could take the place of his late wife.

Hazel was not worthy of that kind of love or devotion.

She didn't want to get hurt again.

She was so scared of that.

She needed to build up her defenses better, even though her heart didn't really want to.

Come on, Hazel. You can do this.

Only when it came to Caleb she was so weak.

Apparently her subconscious thought so too, because she usually didn't fall asleep around just anyone.

"I'm so sorry," she said groggily, trying to sit up straighter. "I didn't mean to do that."

"It's okay. I'm used to front seat nappers. Lizzie often drifts off during long car trips. I am glad that you've woken up though, as I don't know exactly where you live."

"Jade Street. I'm just around the corner from the center and the hospital. I live above a coffee shop."

"I know the place."

"That's my little apartment. It's not exactly the most exciting place, but it's mine and it's convenient."

"We should be there in no time. I'll help you carry up your equipment."

"Actually, we should probably stop at the center first so I can take it there. They are my birthing kits, and I'll have to replenish them and sterilize the equipment. If I have to walk to work tomorrow, then I don't want to have to lug two large duffels with me."

"I understand, but tomorrow is Saturday. Your center is open?"

"Not for regular appointments, but babies don't take the weekend off," she said lightly.

"That's true. I'm not on rotation, so it's my day off and Lizzie is staying with friends."

He sounded so sad and though she knew she shouldn't, she offered, "Well, if you want to hold on to the bags, you can bring them by the center tomorrow morning for me and I'll buy you breakfast."

"You bought dinner tonight."

"Yeah, but I still feel like I owe you for driving me."

"I'll gladly drop the bags off to you tomorrow. Maybe if you don't get called out, we can do something together?"

Her heart skipped a beat. Was he asking her out?

She didn't know quite how to answer that.

She knew what she had to say. She should say no, she should resist him. The problem was, she liked being with him. Even though they'd had to attend a birth and diagnose quints together, it wasn't the work that she enjoyed the most.

It was the company.

Bria had her own patients, and they had both been so busy recently.

It would be nice to get out and do something with someone else.

"What were you thinking of?" she asked.

"Have you been to Multnomah Falls? I mean your center is named after them."

Hazel smiled. "No, I haven't actually been there."

"Well, it's only thirty minutes outside of Portland. It's spectacular with all the leaves starting to bud. Every season has its merits."

"I would like that."

Caleb pulled up in front of her apartment. "What time will you be at the center?"

"Around ten?"

He nodded. "I'll bring you back your equipment then."

"Sounds good. Thank you again." She got out of the car quickly.

She waved as Caleb drove away, leaving her standing there.

Still in shock.

What was happening here?

* * *

Caleb hefted the two duffel bags out of the trunk of his car and carried them to the center. He didn't know what possessed him to invite Hazel out today. All night he'd tossed and turned about his decision, and part of him was trying to figure out a way to get out of it.

It was only a small part though, because there was a much louder part of him that was lonely and really wanted to spend more time with her.

There was an off chance that their day would be interrupted by her need to attend a birth, but he couldn't rely on that as an excuse not to go.

What else did he have to do today?

There was a bunch of emails from several members of the board of directors, particularly Timothy Russell, who was asking for yet another meeting, and for Caleb to provide more facts and figures. He wanted birth rate stats since the Women's Health Center had opened. Something about wanting to investigate the negative impact the opening of the center had had on the hospital.

It was pointless and a waste of time.

Timothy was grasping at straws.

Caleb was ignoring the mounting emails.

They were getting on his nerves.

It annoyed him that the board was clearly trying to sabotage the birthing center. He was so bothered by it, he was beginning to resent being tied to the hospital. Even though the hospital and its staff were stellar.

Timothy Russell had been a problem ever since he'd become chair last year. Even Victor hated him, and the chief of staff didn't hate anyone.

Caleb had no time for this meeting, nor had he pulled together the required information.

He was not looking forward to Monday, but that was Monday's problem.

Today, he didn't want to think about that, because he was simultaneously dreading and excited for his day out with Hazel.

She was waiting for him at the door.

"Right on time," she said.

"I'm always punctual," he replied as he carried the bags in for her.

"Still, there was a part of me that wondered if this was one of the hospital's ploys to whisk away my equipment and force me to leave."

Caleb frowned. "The board of directors may not like you, but I can assure you that the hospital staff isn't that devious. Though I certainly wouldn't put it past the chairman. However, I am not him and I've brought you back your equipment."

Hazel laughed softly. "We'll take it to the sterilization room and I'll repack it."

"Have they figured out what was up with your car?" he asked.

"Yes, it's the alternator. It was towed away yesterday, and Bria texted me to let me know what was happening. I might have to invest in a new to me vehicle soon. I've had Sally for ten years."

Caleb cocked an eyebrow. "Sally?"

"My car," Hazel explained. She undid one of the bags and began washing and sterilizing the equipment.

"I've never named a car before," Caleb stated with a bemused smile.

"You should. It's fun. I get to cuss at something in traffic. Helps keep down the rage in a traffic jam."

Caleb chuckled. "I don't think I have the heart to name my car. I wouldn't know what to call it anyways."

"How about Rex?" Hazel offered.

"That's ridiculous."

"I think people called Rex would argue with that."

After the equipment had been properly sterilized, they finished repacking the bags. She tucked them away, as she currently didn't have a car and wouldn't get hers back until tomorrow, and she told him that she didn't have any patients that were due to deliver any time soon. She had some downtime.

"So, what were you thinking of doing today? Besides just going to the falls?"

"You need to know everything?" he asked.

"I like to be prepared."

He cocked an eyebrow. "How about we just wing it?"

"Whoa."

"What?" he asked.

"Seems kind of relaxed for a surgeon," she teased.

"Must be a bit of my leftover West Coast California vibe then."

Hazel laughed. "Must be. Have to say I like it. The relaxed bit, not the unknown."

"Well, let's get in…in Rex and drive there," he said grudgingly.

She smiled brightly. "I'm so glad that you're warming up to the name."

"I assure you I'm not," he groaned.

They walked out of the center and Hazel locked up.

It was a crisp, cool and misty spring day. It wasn't the best weather for a walk across the bridge by Multnomah Falls, but they could make it work. It had been one of his late wife's favorite places to go.

It had been a long time since Caleb had driven out there.

Lizzie often liked to go when she was a child because Jane had loved it, so Lizzie wanted to feel connected to the mother she never knew. Whenever he brought Lizzie here, he would bury the hurt and the memories deep, deep down, and he never came out here if he absolutely didn't have to.

He wasn't sure what made him think of bringing Hazel out here. For some reason, it didn't seem quite as painful as it had in the past, and he found himself actually looking forward to it for once. It alarmed him how comfortable he was getting with her. She was becoming a part of his life and moving beyond just a colleague. She was becoming something more.

Something he wasn't sure he wanted.

He didn't say much as they drove out of the city and followed the river to Multnomah Falls.

"You've gone all quiet and broody again," Hazel commented.

"Sorry. I was just thinking that it's been some time since I've been out here."

"I've driven by it, but never stopped."

"It was my late wife's favorite place," he said quietly.

"You told me she died in childbirth."

"She did. A pulmonary embolism during her emergency C-section. Her heart stopped, and they couldn't resuscitate her. She lost so much blood and..." He trailed off, because it was a hard thing to talk about. "I'm very mindful of blood clots during emergency caesareans for my clients."

And he was.

When he'd returned to school after his wife died, it had been hard for him for one second to pick up a scalpel, to focus on what he needed to do to become a doctor, but he had managed to compartmentalize it all. He'd put away his own trauma about how his wife had died on the operating table.

He'd concentrated on his work, the patients and

the fact that he wasn't going to allow another woman's partner to feel the same kind of pain that he'd felt when he was told that Jane was gone.

"Childbirth is a scary thing," Hazel said quietly. "We lost a mother during one of my first rotations as a midwife in training. It was crushing. We did everything we could. She gave birth in a hospital, but there was no stopping the bleeding. It almost, for one moment, deterred me."

"Yet you persisted," he said.

"As did you."

They shared a smile.

"Have you ever been married?" he asked suddenly. He was a bit uncomfortable talking about it, but he was surprised that a beautiful, intelligent, vibrant woman like Hazel Rees was unattached.

"I came close. Once. He was a surgeon. We met at the hospital I worked at after I became a nurse practitioner. He pursued the general surgery program, and I was trying to save up to study midwifery. We were both busy and then... I found him with another woman. In a closet. It was absolutely soul crushingly painful. I decided then I would focus on my own dreams. I became a midwife, worked in a hospital in southern Arizona for a couple of years, then focused on opening this center with my best friend."

"He was an idiot," Caleb murmured. "I'm glad you didn't let him deter you from pursuing your dreams."

"My dad would've kicked my butt if I'd given up. He taught me to fight for what I want." There was a hint of sadness to her voice.

And he couldn't help but wonder what it was, what was causing her sadness.

It's not your business.

Except he badly wanted to comfort her. He'd thought she was too young to carry wounds as deep as his own, but maybe he was wrong about that. Inside that professional exterior of hers, she had been living with pain just like he had.

And he hated that she'd had to do that.

She deserved so much better than her ex.

You're better than he is.

He pushed that thought away immediately.

"You father sounds like a smart man." He was trying to change the subject and steer it away from the reminder of lost love.

Hazel smiled. "He is, but don't tell him that! He'll never stop gloating over it."

Caleb chuckled. "My father couldn't care less about my desire to pursue medicine. He wanted me to be in with the Hollywood crowd."

"Why did you go into obstetrics?"

"My wife. I had planned on being a general surgeon, but when she died in childbirth I wanted to devote my life to saving others from what I went through."

"That's admirable."

"I don't regret it." He smiled. "How about you?"

"My sister. She was pushed through the hospital system so fast and had some complications after the birth of my niece. I wanted to provide more personalized care for women like her."

"I think we both have pretty good reasons."

A blush tinged her cheeks. "Some more common ground."

They neared the parking lot of the falls. Caleb found a parking spot. It was busy, but then this site was always busy as it was one of the more popular places to visit in Oregon. They picked up a map and started the steep climb up to the Benson Bridge.

There was a definite chill to the air, which was unusual for May.

Hazel reached into her pocket and pulled out a woolen beanie and pulled it down over her head. It was multicolored and looked quite monstrous. He couldn't help but chuckle.

"What?" she asked.

"Your beanie. It's quite vibrant, much like your toe socks. Just hairier."

"My grandma made this for me when my father first got stationed to Alaska. It was to keep me warm, and it always has. It's made of alpaca. She had several of them on her ranch in New Mexico."

"Don't tell me you ate those too?" he asked.

"What? Why would you assume that?" she choked out.

"You've eaten a seal."

"Not a whole seal and I told you why!"

He grinned. "Okay, you did. I'm sorry."

"Thank you. The most I did was shear a few alpacas for wool."

"Sheared them?" he asked.

"Yes."

"You never cease to amaze me. You're quite surprising."

"As are you."

"Hardly," he muttered.

"Your mother was in a Bond movie. That trumps everything."

They smiled together. And all the tension and sadness caused by their previous conversation melted away in an instant.

The bridge was cluttered with groups of people wanting to take pictures of the dramatic falls cascading down a high mountain cliff. It was truly spectacular, but they walked away from the crowds trying to get selfies and post things to their social media.

Instead, they found a quiet corner of the bridge to gaze up at the water.

The mist was sprinkling moisture on her face, and she was smiling up at the water.

Not complaining about the cold or the damp.

Much like Jane, but also different.

There was a real zest for life in Hazel.

It had been a long time since he had seen such a spark of vitality in someone. It just softened him, and he found he really wanted to take a chance on her. Baggage be damned. Hazel made him feel alive and not so lonely. He frowned. She was shaking; he could hear her teeth chattering!

"Are you cold?" he asked.

"A bit. I thought the hat would help, but there's quite the chill in the air. It's spring, so logically it should be warmer."

Without thinking he opened his large overcoat and pulled her close against him. She gasped, staring up at him. Her cheeks were rosy, and he could see how long her lashes were. Her body was so warm flushed against him, so soft. He hadn't been thinking when he'd made the gesture, and now his pulse was thundering between his ears. All he wanted to do was kiss her. To taste her lips. The temptation was overwhelming.

Hazel didn't step away, and he could smell her delicious perfume.

Vanilla.

Like something sweet baking.

"Hazel," he said gruffly.

"Yes," she whispered.

"I would very much like to kiss you now."

"I'd like that too."

He didn't need any more encouragement. He bent down and kissed her lightly on her soft, supple lips, drinking in the honeyed taste of her. She didn't push him away. Instead, her arms came around him and he cupped her rosy cheeks, kissing her deeper.

He wanted her closer. His body was thrumming with need, and all he wanted was her.

And then he realized what he was doing, and he reluctantly broke off the kiss and stepped away. This couldn't happen.

They were professional colleagues and nothing more. And now he knew she'd been hurt badly before. He wouldn't be the one to hurt her again. It was far too risky.

He hadn't been thinking straight.

"Hazel, I'm sorry. That shouldn't have happened. My apologies."

She nodded, her cheeks pink. "No need to apologize, but you're right that shouldn't have happened. It can't happen again."

CHAPTER SEVEN

HAZEL DIDN'T KNOW what had come over her. She was staring up at the falls and thinking about her late grandmother and freezing. It wasn't as cold as Alaska, but she had spent the last couple of years with her sister in southern Arizona where it was considerably warmer and drier. She was instantly regretting her choice to dress nicely rather than sensibly. Jeans just didn't cut it when it was cold and damp out, but she'd wanted to dress a little bit more stylishly knowing that she was going to see Caleb.

She had clearly lost her mind, because she would've never done that before.

She'd spent years in Alaska, and she knew exactly how to dress for the weather.

Up there, dressing for the weather meant life or death. And she didn't know why she was trying to impress Caleb so badly.

Nothing could happen between them, even though she wanted it to. She was fighting with disaster, but it seemed she couldn't help herself.

She had been trying to hold back the teeth chattering, and then he'd opened up his coat to embrace her and she'd stepped into his arms without thinking. It just felt like the most natural thing in the world to do.

Wrapped up in his arms she felt warm and safe. Like she was supposed to be there.

Like she belonged.

And then he'd asked to kiss her and she'd melted.

Caleb's kiss had seared her soul. It made her toes curl in her boots and her body combust. The primitive part of her brain wanted much more, but the logical side was screaming at her that this was all wrong. She'd willfully ignored that part.

Thankfully, he'd broken off the kiss.

She was still shaking, and it wasn't because of the cold. It was because of him and that spectacular kiss.

She was trying to get ahold of her emotions, her senses, but right now she felt like a big pile of goo and she couldn't even focus on the falls right in front of her.

"Why don't we head down to the little restaurant and get some coffee?" he suggested.

"Coffee sounds good."

Anything to get her mind off what just happened.

Hazel usually didn't let herself get too carried away around men, even the ones she was attracted to. She was in control of herself, and she was always careful. She wasn't going to let another Mark into her life. She had learned her lesson. Staying in control was a way to protect her heart from pain.

From disappointment.

She operated better this way.

So what was it about Caleb that destroyed the defenses that she had carefully cultivated for so long?

It was seriously annoying.

She was still a little chilly, and as they walked down to the little coffee shop off the parking lot, she wished she could crawl back into his warm arms and be wrapped up. Safe and sound.

Stop that.

It was very dangerous thinking.

The coffee shop wasn't too busy, and they grabbed some hot coffee and found a little table in the corner, away from the rest of the tourists but where they could still see the waterfalls. She cupped the warm cup in her hands.

It was a way to ground her.

"I'm sorry if I overstepped," Caleb said awkwardly, breaking through the silence.

"No. You weren't the only one who overstepped our boundaries. You weren't the only willing participant. You asked and I said yes."

He half smiled. "Still, we're supposed to be colleagues."

"Exactly." Hazel swallowed the lump in her throat.

She completely agreed with what he was saying, but why did it feel like a slap in the face? She wasn't sure, but some stubborn part of her knew this was for the best.

It really was.

She wanted to have a good working partnership with him.

It would benefit the patients of the Multnomah Falls Women's Health Center in the long run to be on good terms with the head of obstetrics at St. Raymond's.

So even though it felt like a complete gut punch and every part of her body was telling her to kiss him again, it was for the best.

Completely.

If they got together and it didn't work out, it would make things between them awkward.

And he had a daughter.

A grown-up child, to be sure, but he still was a father and that daughter of his was pregnant. She was pretty sure Lizzie still hadn't told her father what was going on. Hazel couldn't tell him. She was the young woman's midwife.

But she didn't like keeping secrets or lying.

Mark had done both with all his affairs and lying about why he was jilted. She abhorred lying, and it ate away at her that she was keeping this huge secret from him. Caleb deserved to know; only professionally her hands were tied.

It was all getting too complicated. She just wanted things to be simple again.

She had to convince Lizzie to tell her father the truth. Caleb would understand. She was sure of it. If Caleb knew, then she wouldn't have to keep this secret from him.

She was going to suggest that they go home when someone came running into the restaurant. It was a highway patrolman.

"There's a massive pileup on the highway. A logging truck lost control. There are several people injured. Is anyone here a doctor?" the panicked man asked. "We can't get emergency services in on the ground yet, and a fog bank is delaying helicopters."

"I am," Caleb said, standing up.

Hazel nodded. "We can help."

"Great," the officer said, relieved. "I'll take you to the accident. If anyone else has any kind of first aid or triage training, we really need your assistance."

A couple more patrons raised their hands.

They followed the highway patrolman out. There were a couple of squad cars. He sent off the first aid volunteers with another patrolman and then turned to them.

"I have the worst victims. The logging truck hit a couple of cars. I need the medical professionals right at the scene. It's pretty bad."

Caleb's lips pressed together in a thin line. "I'm an obstetrician, but I'll help any way I can."

"I'm a midwife, but I'm a nurse practitioner too. As long as you have first aid kits, we can help," Hazel said, hoping that her voice didn't shake. It had been a long time since she did a rotation in the emergency room.

The fast pace of trauma never did suit her, but

this wasn't the time or place to quibble. Lives were on the line.

There was a rock in her stomach, but she pushed all of her nerves out the door when the patrol car turned on its sirens and they headed up the highway a short distance. As they rounded the corner, she could see smoke billowing into the sky.

"Oh, my God," Caleb whispered.

Her heart skipped a beat, and her adrenaline kicked in at the sight of scattered twisted metal and cars. The logging truck had spewed its load across the entire width of the highway and the truck itself was lying on its side, flames billowing outward.

The patrolman stopped and they got out of the car.

"The driver is the worst. He's pinned, and we're waiting for the fire crew to get here and use the Jaws of Life on him, but the car he hit, the driver is lying over here and he's in pretty bad shape."

"Take me to him," Caleb said, whipping off his coat and putting it into the patrol car. Hazel followed him as he rolled up the sleeves of his white cotton shirt.

The man was lying on his back, barely conscious, and his pregnant wife was kneeling next to him, weeping.

Hazel went to her.

"Ma'am?" Hazel asked gently. "I'm a midwife. Can I check you?"

"I'm fine," the woman said. "I'm only seven

months along. I'm okay, the baby is kicking. I'm fine. It's my husband who's hurt." The woman was rambling, clearly in shock.

"Dr. Norris is going to take care of your husband. What's your name?" Hazel asked, kneeling next to the distraught woman.

"Jennifer," she said, not tearing her gaze from her husband.

Hazel could see a small laceration on her temple that was bandaged, but most likely needed to be stitched.

"Jennifer, how about we let the doctor see to him? I would really like to check you over," Hazel suggested.

The woman finally looked at her. "Okay."

Hazel guided her away and grabbed one of the blankets that a highway patrol man brought her. She wrapped Jennifer in the blanket to keep her warm and had her take the seat in the open door of a squad car.

"I'm going to check your pulse, if that's okay?"

Jennifer nodded, distracted.

Hazel took her pulse and it was thready.

"Can I feel a kick?" Hazel asked.

"Of course."

Hazel placed her hand on Jennifer's belly. It was hard, and Hazel felt the beginning of a contraction. Jennifer's body was pumping so much adrenaline through her that Jennifer couldn't feel it.

Hazel worried her bottom lip.

Jennifer was going into preterm labor.

The baby did kick, but there was nothing more she could do. There was no way to stop her labor.

Then Hazel noticed the blood running down Jennifer's leg. It was either from a cut or it was from the baby. She really hoped it was from a cut and not the womb.

Hazel heard the wail of an ambulance siren. She glanced over her shoulder to see the flashing lights wind their way through the tangle of cars, and she breathed a sigh of relief.

The first paramedic crew headed toward Caleb, and the second crew went to the truck driver as the fire crew was fast on the heels of the ambulances.

Caleb finished up with his instructions to the paramedics, and they loaded up Jennifer's husband in the back of the ambulance. Jennifer began to groan, and Hazel began to time the pain and heavy breathing. The contractions were close together. There was no denying that Jennifer was in labor.

"Where are they taking Teddy?" Jennifer asked.

"To the hospital. He'll be fine. Jennifer, you're in labor," Hazel said gently.

"What?" Then Jennifer winced and clutched her belly. "No, I can't be. I'm only thirty weeks. It's too early."

Jennifer's water broke and Hazel saw blood, so not from a cut then. She winced internally.

Caleb looked up as the ambulance with Teddy took off toward the hospital.

Hazel waved him over.

"What's wrong?" Caleb asked.

"This is Teddy's wife, Jennifer. She's thirty weeks along and is in labor."

Caleb nodded. "Has her water broken?"

"Yes," Hazel said quietly. "There's blood."

"Grab a first aid kit and a blanket from the back of the squad car. I've delivered these extreme preemies before. I don't have what I need here to stop the birth," he said.

"Agreed." Hazel turned to Jennifer. "This is Dr. Norris. He's an obstetrician from St. Raymond's."

"My husband?" Jennifer asked wildly.

"He's stable and on the way to Portland," Caleb answered patiently, reassuring her again as it was clear the poor woman wasn't focusing on details at a time like this. "I need to check on you and your baby."

Jennifer nodded, and they got her settled back into the squad car.

Hazel got the supplies they would need and helped get Jennifer's skirt off. Her water had definitely broken, and there was a bloody show. Hazel draped her for modesty as best she could and then climbed into the back of the patrol car to support Jennifer, who was terrified and in a lot of pain.

"You're ten centimeters," Caleb said.

"Already?" Hazel asked with a raised eyebrow.

Caleb nodded. "Adrenaline, the accident, have speeded it up."

"I can't have this baby without Teddy here," Jennifer cried.

"You're going to have to push your baby out with the next contraction," Caleb stated firmly, but gently.

"It's too soon," Jennifer wailed piteously.

"I know, sweetie, but you have to do this. Your baby isn't going to wait for the emergency services," Hazel said encouragingly.

Jennifer nodded, crying as she pushed with the contraction.

Caleb frowned. "Your baby is breech and I'm going to turn them. Try to stay as still as you can for me."

Jennifer winced, and Hazel leaned over to help Caleb by turning Jennifer's abdomen to help with the breech position. He didn't have to tell her to do it. She knew what to do. Their gazes locked, and she could see the gratitude in his eyes.

"There we go," Caleb said.

Hazel held on to Jennifer's hands as she no longer needed to push on her abdomen.

"Come on, push," Hazel urged.

Jennifer's legs shook, and she gave one large push and Caleb caught the small, wrinkly preemie in his hands.

"It's a boy," he said as he quickly cut the cord.

Hazel made sure that Jennifer was comfortable and went through the other passenger door to go and help Caleb. The baby wasn't breathing.

Another ambulance pulled up, and the emergency services team opened their doors.

"We need an incubator and oxygen," Hazel said. "Thirty-week preemie has just been delivered. Also need a large bore intravenous, fluids and antibiotics for the mother."

"Right away," the paramedic said.

Caleb had wrapped the preemie in a blanket and was gently massaging the little boy's back. Willing the early bird to breath.

The baby was so tiny in his large hands.

It made Hazel's heart skip a beat.

There was a thin cry. So quiet, like a cat, almost, as the little boy gasped for his first breaths. The paramedics brought over the incubator, and Caleb helped them load in the tiny infant. Hazel returned to Jennifer, who was beginning to get uncomfortable as she delivered the placenta.

There was a lot of bleeding and Hazel suspected a tear, which could be from the accident.

Caleb returned and saw what she saw.

"I need to get her into surgery as soon as possible. I'll need to go with them to St. Raymond's," he said.

"I'll take your car back to Portland," Hazel offered. "I don't need to go. Just take care of her."

Caleb nodded, but he didn't look her in the eye.

They hadn't really had a chance to talk about what had happened at the falls.

Maybe it was best they didn't. They could just forget about their kiss and go on.

"Thank you for your help. I didn't have to tell you what to do."

"I know. It's kind of my job," she said, grinning.

He smiled at her, his blue-gray eyes twinkling, and then he leaned down and her breath caught in her throat, thinking he was going to kiss her again. Her pulse quickened.

He moved away quickly. "The keys are in my jacket."

Hazel nodded, feeling a bit foolish now thinking he'd been going to kiss her again. "Go. Save a life."

"I will see you later."

She nodded again and watched as he climbed into the back of the ambulance with Jennifer and the little boy. Her pulse was racing as she watched the ambulance race away.

"Ms. Rees?" the patrolman asked.

"Yes," she said. "More injured?"

"Some minor stuff. I could use your help."

"I'm glad to help. Let's go."

And she was. She followed the patrolman into the fray, watching as the flashing lights disappeared down the highway.

Caleb's kiss felt like it was still burning on her lips. His kiss had been like a promise. One she knew that he most likely wouldn't keep. She wasn't going to get her hopes up. It was safer for her heart this way, even though there was a little part of her that wanted to hope.

There was a small part of her that wanted him.

Even though it put her heart at risk.

It terrified her.

Hazel got back from the accident scene and carried Caleb's jacket to his office, but when she left and headed back out of the hospital she found Mrs. Jameson wandering the halls.

Clutching her abdomen.

Oh. No.

"Mrs. Jameson? Tara?" Hazel asked, coming over.

"My water broke. Wilfred is out of town. My mom is with my little girl. I'm alone." Tara winced. "It hurts."

"Come on. Let's get you to labor and delivery."

Hazel found a wheelchair and got Tara settled. She rushed her down to the labor and delivery floor.

"Ms. Rees?" Janet, the head nurse familiar with her, asked.

"Janet, this is Tara Jameson. She's para two, gravida one and thirty-five weeks pregnant. She had a low transverse C-section three years ago. Her contractions are five minutes apart. Dr. Norris needs to be paged."

Janet took over the wheelchair. "He's still in surgery on that uterine rupture."

"Okay."

"I'll have another nurse get you some scrubs," Janet said. "And we'll help Mrs. Jameson."

"I want Hazel," Tara said. "She's my midwife and she knows my birth plan."

"Of course," Janet said. "We'll get her ready to help you, and we'll let Dr. Norris know."

"I'll be with you soon."

Another nurse handed Hazel a set of scrubs, and Hazel made her way down to the staff change room.

She was exhausted, but this was part of the job. She had to put everything from her mind.

Even that kiss.

Hazel changed and then headed back to the labor and delivery suite.

Hovering outside was Timothy Russell, who had clearly gotten wind that Mrs. Jameson had come in. She paused and he turned to look at her, sneering.

"Where is Dr. Norris?" Timothy demanded.

"In surgery." Hazel tried to move past him.

"Where do you think you're going?"

"To deliver my patient's baby. She requested me."

"You don't have privileges here."

"So give me privileges. Either way, I'm her midwife and I'm going to help her. You have a problem, take it up with the patient who is in a lot of pain right now—see where it gets you." Hazel pushed past him.

Janet was trying to calm Tara down, but the labor was progressing quickly.

"Her contractions are coming more frequently," Janet stated.

Hazel pulled on gloves. "I'm going to check you, Tara. Okay?"

Tara was crying and Hazel did an internal. The baby was head down, and she was eight centimeters dilated. It wouldn't be long now, and it was too late for pain relief. What she had to watch for now was the baby's heart rate, and excessive bleeding.

Both signs that the vaginal birth after caesarean section was failing.

Janet got monitors on Tara to watch the heart rate and her contractions, and Hazel helped get Tara hooked up to an IV for liquids, so she didn't get dehydrated.

It wasn't long before Caleb came into the room. In a fresh change of scrubs, bags under his eyes.

"I came as soon as my surgery was over," he said, pulling on gloves. "How is she?"

"She's eight centimeters dilated. Baby's heart rate is good," Hazel stated.

Caleb nodded. "I'm going to check you, Tara, okay?"

Tara nodded.

Hazel held her while Caleb did his exam. "She's fully dilated now. There's a bit more blood than I'm comfortable with."

Hazel stood next to him and looked. "You don't think she needs to go into surgery?"

Caleb shook his head. "We'll watch, but so far, no."

The baby was coming fast, just like the last delivery. This baby was early too, but closer to the due date than Jennifer's little boy. Their main concern now was Tara.

"With your next contraction, I need you to push, Tara!" Hazel urged.

Tara nodded and pushed, crying out.

The baby began to crown.

There was no sign of the shoulder being stuck, which could often be a sign of a failed vaginal birth after caesarean, and the heart rate was still favorable.

Hazel took point next to Caleb.

Both of them encouraging Tara.

A few more pushes and her little boy came into the world, screaming and shouting.

"It's a boy," Caleb announced.

Tara was crying, and Hazel took the baby as Caleb cut the cord. She placed the boy against his mother's chest, so he could get skin to skin contact and covered his back with a blanket.

Caleb watched for the placenta to be delivered.

If there was a real problem with uterine rupture or the placenta imbedding itself too deeply, they would be able to tell when it was delivered.

A few minutes later, Tara's placenta was delivered whole and everything was going smoothly. It was a successful vaginal birth after caesarean section.

"Thank you both, so much."

"My pleasure," Hazel said.

Caleb smiled and nodded. "I'll come and check on you later."

Hazel was a bit annoyed that he only referred to himself coming and checking on her, but she wasn't going to get into an argument with him in front of the patient.

She helped Janet clean up and then headed out into the hall after Caleb, who'd left a few minutes before.

When she got into the hallway, she saw Caleb talking to Timothy Russell.

And she knew it was about her. She didn't know what they were saying. There was a lot of frowning and nodding going on.

It made her stomach twist in a bunch of knots.

Timothy came over to her. "You need to leave now, Ms. Rees. It's after hours."

Caleb stood there, not saying anything. His face just a professional mask.

"Of course."

There was no point in arguing.

The board of directors had spoken and Caleb hadn't said much, but she figured his hands were tied too.

Or perhaps he just didn't care about her work as much as he said he did.

Once more she was falling into a trap of trusting again, even though she didn't really want to believe it this time.

CHAPTER EIGHT

IT HAD BEEN two weeks since Caleb had seen Hazel and they'd delivered their vaginal birth after caesarean section patient successfully. Mrs. Jameson was doing well as was her little boy.

After he'd completed Jennifer's uterine repair surgery, he'd wanted to talk to Hazel about their kiss, but Tara Jameson went into labor.

They didn't get a chance to talk about it, and then Timothy Russell had been seriously annoyed that Hazel was there.

It was ridiculous and he'd been cross about it, but then Hazel had left St. Raymond's.

It was the last he'd seen of her and though he should be relieved by the space, he'd missed her.

It had been a long time since he'd missed someone like this. It alarmed him because the only other woman who had made him feel like that had been Jane. Since his wife died he'd been attracted to other women, but he'd had no drive to do much about it, other than the odd fling. With Hazel it was so different, and it was apparent to him that she had been just as freaked out by what had happened at the falls.

It was better to get some distance from one another.

Wasn't it?

He groaned and stared at all the reports in front of him. All the facts and figures the board had requested.

Now he was finally forced to hand them over, but he really didn't want to.

Bringing money to the hospital was all that mattered to the board, not necessarily the work that he was doing, that the rest of the hospital staff was doing.

Caleb could only delay the inevitable for so long, and two weeks was all the board had been willing to wait. So as he made his way to Timothy's office he girded his loins for a serious talk.

He didn't know what Timothy wanted now, but Caleb couldn't help but wonder if he was getting some flak from investors. Caleb was so over it all. He would walk away, except he had Lizzie to take care of.

Yes, Lizzie was in college, but he was helping her with tuition so she could focus on studying.

This job was his stability, and he did still love his work here. He just hated the politics of it all.

He straightened his spine and knocked on Timothy's door.

"Come in."

Caleb opened the door and shut it as Timothy stood and smiled.

"Caleb, so good to see you. Please have a seat."

Caleb took the aforementioned seat. "I'm sorry

that I had to postpone this meeting. These last two weeks have been incredibly busy."

"I know. You helped out at that traffic accident. It brought us a lot of good press. That couple wouldn't have made it without your help, Dr. Norris. And everyone in the accident survived. Even the little baby. How is the baby?"

"Very well. He's under Dr. Prince's care in the neonatal intensive care unit."

Timothy smiled. "Good. Good. As I said, the press on that was so good for St. Raymond's."

"Medicine and saving lives are good for the hospital. As is working with other health care practitioners."

Timothy's eyes narrowed. "The midwives you mean?"

"Yes. Hazel Rees helped me deliver that baby too. And assisted me in the successful delivery of Mrs. Jameson's child. Your tirade on them is not good press."

"It may not be, but that birthing center threatens our financial future."

Caleb sighed. "I don't know what you expect me to do about it. I'm the head of obstetrics and my focus should be on patients, not worrying about a midwife clinic across the road that's not breaking the law."

"I understand."

Timothy folded his hands on his desk, and Caleb

caught a glimpse of his expensive watch. Everything about Timothy was meant to intimidate.

Caleb wasn't so easily pushed around.

"So then I don't see the problem," Caleb stated.

"The problem is Mrs. Patterson."

Caleb frowned. "Why is Mrs. Patterson a problem?"

"The board of directors and myself are concerned that Mrs. Patterson still has Ms. Rees listed as her main practitioner."

Caleb shrugged. "And?"

"She won't be delivering quints over there. She'll deliver them here. Your reports state the obvious outcome."

"What does it matter who the main practitioner is listed as being? As long as the babies and Mrs. Patterson survive."

"It matters to the press."

Caleb saw red and clenched his fists, trying to calm down. "So the board is simply concerned that Mrs. Patterson is Hazel Rees's patient?"

"Yes."

"Well, Hazel did refer Mrs. Patterson to me. So technically it is true. Hazel Rees is the main practitioner on the case."

"The board doesn't want Hazel Rees to have hospital privileges here."

Caleb was shocked, but also not really. "You mean you don't. But you are aware that decision puts lives in danger, Timothy. We have always given privileges to midwives here at St. Raymond's."

Timothy sighed. "The midwives having privileges undercuts the hospital. How better it would be, for all of us, money wise, to have you as Mrs. Patterson's main practitioner, not Hazel. Mrs. Jameson is already telling her friends, wealthy friends I might add, that Hazel delivered her child."

"This conversation is ridiculous."

"I assure you, it's not. Mrs. Patterson is carrying quintuplets, and we would like you, as the head of obstetrics, to be the main practitioner on such a high-profile case."

"Mrs. Patterson is not a PR stunt. She's a patient and I won't jeopardize her health."

"You know with high-order births that the best chance of the mother and the babies surviving is having them in a hospital."

Caleb sighed. "I know, but I won't force Mrs. Patterson or Hazel into that decision. However, both the patient and Hazel Rees are quite aware of the complications, and I will not deny Mrs. Patterson health care just because she lists Hazel Rees as her main practitioner. The babies will likely be born here with my help and Hazel's. Hazel will still officially be the main practitioner."

Timothy nodded slowly. "I see."

"I don't think you do, but as long as I'm head

of obstetrics, the midwives will be allowed access and privileges here, understood?"

"I'm glad you have made your position known. I look forward to reading your report," Timothy said calmly, but Caleb got the distinct impression this wasn't over. He took that as his cue to leave and he was glad to.

As he left Timothy's office, he ran into Victor.

"Hey, I've been looking for you," Victor said.

"Have you?"

"Yes. You haven't checked your email, have you?" Victor asked.

"No. I've been busy."

Distracted was more like it.

Constantly thinking about Hazel. Worried about Lizzie, who seemed to be catching the flu, but insisted she was fine.

There was a lot going on.

"There's a lecture on high-order births that you're supposed to attend in Seattle tomorrow."

Caleb paused. "What?"

"You signed up to go a few months ago. The hospital got you a hotel room and booked your flight, for tonight. The lecture is tomorrow morning."

"I have to attend this lecture?"

Victor nodded. "You do. You requested to go, and the hospital is footing the bill."

"I completely forgot."

"You've been a bit scatterbrained lately. Are you okay?" Victor asked with concern.

"I am. Truly. I would still like to attend."

"Well, the details are all in your email."

"Thanks, Victor."

Victor turned to walk away. "Oh, I saw your daughter waiting for you outside your office."

"Lizzie's there? She's supposed to be in class."

Victor shrugged. "She said she'd wait."

"Thanks, Victor."

Caleb made his way back to his office and sure enough Lizzie was outside, waiting for him. She looked uncomfortable and a bit pale.

Immediately he was concerned.

"Lizzie?"

"Hey, Dad," she said.

"Are you okay?" he asked, sitting next to her.

"Fine. Just tired. Midterms took a toll on me."

Although, he didn't think it was midterms only. He touched her forehead, but she didn't have a fever. She just felt clammy.

"I'm supposed to fly to Seattle tonight. Why don't I cancel?"

"No, Dad. You have to do your job. I just wanted to stop by and see you, but I didn't realize you were leaving tonight. I have class later." Lizzie leaned against him.

"What class?" he asked, relishing the small moment of affection she'd used to give him more frequently when she was smaller, when she would often want to cuddle with him. It had been some time since she just wanted to see him.

He hated to see her grown up. Even though those days of juggling school and a newborn alone were hard, he sometimes missed them.

"Anatomy," she groused. "Cadaver night. Not looking forward to it."

"You'll do great. And if you want to go to med school still…"

"I don't though. I want to be a midwife."

He smiled. "I know. You've told me. Don't worry. I just want you to be happy."

Lizzie sighed, then stood up. "Thanks, Dad. I better prep for class."

"Be safe."

"I will. When will you be back from Seattle?"

"Sunday. I think."

Lizzie nodded. "Okay."

Caleb watched her walk away. He was worried about her, and he was worried about leaving her.

Maybe Hazel could keep an eye on Lizzie. He called her cell number, but it went straight to voice mail. So he texted instead, but it just sat there.

Unread.

She was ignoring him after their kiss and it hurt a bit, but she was justified in being upset with him after he hadn't discussed it with her afterward. It was best that it was all forgotten.

If he wanted to protect his heart, he would have to stop thinking about Hazel Rees and how much he was falling for her.

* * *

Hazel stared out of her hotel room at the Space Needle. She checked her phone, but there was no message. Not that she was expecting anything. She hadn't heard from Caleb in a couple of weeks, and even though the logical side of her brain was telling her that it was good, she'd missed him.

It was like this hole, this ache in her soul.

After the successful VBAC of Mrs. Jameson and the confrontation with Timothy Russell, she was upset that Caleb had stood there and not said anything to defend her.

Of course, she hadn't exactly given him time to say anything.

She'd just left.

She had been so angry, hurt, frustrated, not least of all because she and Caleb also hadn't talked about the kiss they'd shared.

That had been the most stressful thing. She couldn't stop thinking about that kiss. She was angry at herself for letting herself kiss him and be so affected by it.

She closed her eyes and touched her lips. She could still feel his mouth against hers. Her body tingled just thinking about his strong arms around her.

She was so distracted, which was very unlike her.

She'd almost forgotten about this symposium and the lecture she'd wanted to attend about high-

order births, until the notification about her flight
had pinged her.

Maybe some time in Seattle would get her mind
off Caleb and his kisses.

And how ridiculous the chairman of the board
was. Maybe it had been a huge mistake to build
across from St. Raymond's.

No. It's not and you know it.

It wasn't Caleb's fault. It was the hospital board's,
she told herself, but there was a small nagging part
of her that didn't quite trust him completely. She'd
seen Timothy and Caleb's discussion, but didn't
know what it was about and Caleb's face had been
so cool when he'd looked at her afterward. A professional wall had been dropped. Was he truly
being honest with her?

You're not being honest with him.

She did know something important about his
daughter, but that wasn't her secret to tell. Even
though keeping it from Caleb it was eating her
alive.

Lizzie had to tell her father soon.

What Hazel needed to do was protect her heart
and her business.

No money hungry chairman of the board was
going to edge out Bria and her. They had worked
too hard to get where they were now.

Hazel sighed and tore her gaze away from the
Space Needle and the city of Seattle, which was
waking up on this hazy, late spring morning.

There was fog rolling in, which was usual for Seattle, though she'd been hoping for some sun.

So she was glad that she was going to spend all day locked in a lecture.

It wouldn't make her feel so bad for missing out on a beautiful day.

She finished getting ready and left her hotel room. She made sure her door was locked and headed to the elevator, glancing at her phone to make sure that she had time to grab some coffee before heading to the lecture.

The elevator dinged and the doors opened. She walked on and stopped dead in her tracks at the other occupant of the elevator.

"Caleb?" she asked in confusion.

Caleb glanced up from his phone and stood up straight. "Hazel?"

The elevator closed behind her. "What're you doing here?"

"I'm attending a lecture by Dr. Marquez on high-order births today at the insistence of my chief of staff. I had forgotten that I'd asked to go. What're you doing here?"

"Attending the same symposium apparently," she said.

"Well…good."

She stood next to him in awkward silence as the elevator made more stops and more people got on.

He was so close to her. This was not going to help with her resolution to keep herself from him emotionally and maintain her walls. It was easier when she didn't see him. At least that's what she told herself.

Being next to him in such a confined space, she could recall the warmth of his arms around her, the scent of him.

Spicy and masculine.

The strength and security of his embrace was still fresh in her mind.

She had to get control of herself.

"I haven't seen you in a couple of weeks," he said offhandedly.

"I've been busy. I had to check on Clarissa and Jade."

"Jade?"

"Her baby girl."

He nodded. "Nice name."

"I think so too."

"How is the baby's clavicle?"

"Healing really well."

"Good."

Someone else got on and they just stood there. Side by side, saying nothing, but her palms suddenly felt very sweaty.

Finally at the main lobby every one filtered off and they were still standing there, neither of them moving.

"I was on my way to get coffee. Would you like to join me?" she asked.

"Yes. That sounds acceptable," he said stiffly. "I will need something to keep me awake."

They began to walk to the hotel's coffee bar.

"Are you that sure another doctor's lecture will put you to sleep?" she asked.

"I have heard Dr. Kevin Marquez speak before. He's brilliant, but a public speaker he is not."

"Oh, dear. I was going to get decaf. Perhaps I will splurge for the caffeine."

"It's in your best interest." A smile played at the corners of his mouth.

It made her heart beat a bit faster. They were just two colleagues at a lecture.

Out of town.

Even though it was for the best that she resist him, she still missed him. She'd enjoyed their time together, which she'd never thought she would ever think, but there it was. As much as she didn't want miss him.

She did.

And she was glad he was here.

They stood in the seemingly never-ending lineup to the coffee shop.

"I'm sorry that I didn't really speak to you after Mrs. Jameson's delivery. It all took me by surprise. I was so angry with Timothy Russell for asking me to leave."

"Don't worry. I understand…it's ridiculous, really."

"It seems to be that way," she groused.

"Tara Jameson's family is well connected. The board thought delivering her baby at St. Raymond's was good press for them. Just like the accident. They used that to elevate their status in the media too. But that behavior after the VBAC was really immature. I'm sorry Timothy acted that way."

"You say that with such distaste. Not that I blame you."

"It's all well and good that everyone survived. It's fantastic. It's what we strive for as physicians, surgeons, nurses, as health care providers and emergency services, but to use it for PR bothers me deeply. Using it as leverage to get more business or more funding. It just rubs me the wrong way. I was never very good at schmoozing or anything to do with politics in the medical workplace."

"A necessary evil these days, I agree. Funding and grants do help keep beds open, but I know what you mean."

He sighed, and she could tell that he knew exactly what she was talking about. It was so much better being your own boss.

Except their center could use some more funding, and that was a worry that she and Bria had been recently discussing. Bria was a strategist though, and was trying to formulate some kind of fundraiser that Hazel really wanted nothing to do with. Only because Bria was so much better at it. Hazel didn't have the calming demeanor her friend seemed to have.

Hazel would do whatever was needed to help out though.

They placed their respective coffee orders and then headed to the main ballroom of the hotel, which was packed full of other medical professionals.

She was really looking forward to learning all she could about high-order births.

What the complications were, prenatal care of the mother and even learning about postpartum recovery for the mother after the babies were born. A high-order birth was not only precarious for the babies, but also the mother and her body.

She had also seen singleton pregnancies carry complications for the mother postpartum, even years later. Things like adhesions and bladder prolapse. Hazel didn't want to just deliver the babies, she wanted to help the mother afterward too.

It was a service that was seriously lacking.

Especially when it came to postpartum recovery and physiotherapy. She just wanted to be prepared for Mrs. Patterson and she wanted some facts and figures herself, solid information to use against Timothy Russell if he ever tried to deny her access to her patient again.

"Would you like to have dinner tonight?" Caleb asked, as they took seats in the back of the ballroom. It came completely out of the blue, taking her off guard.

"Dinner? Do you think that's wise?"

"Why not?"

Because the last time we were together, we kissed and we can't seem to get past that. There was always heat bubbling under the surface ever since they'd met. Why couldn't she resist him?

"I… I can't think of a reason." She was lying through her teeth. There were so many reasons to say no to him. But right now, staring up into his blue-gray eyes and that strong jaw, those lips that she knew so well, she couldn't think of the million reasons she had gone over in her head for the last couple of weeks.

The reasons why she should resist him, because when it came to Caleb she was so weak.

"Great. I was going to have dinner at the Space Needle alone, but it would be nice to have company and talk about Mrs. Patterson. Go over our game plan and all the scenarios involving the quints."

"A working dinner, at the top of the Space Needle?" she asked.

He nodded. "It's a great view."

"Okay. Around seven then?"

He nodded. "It's a date."

She wanted to say no, it wasn't a date, only she couldn't say anything. She lost her ability in that moment to speak.

Dr. Kevin Marquez walked onto the stage and all further discussion about dinner was done. She had to focus on the guest speaker and the couple of other workshops she planned to attend. Instead, all she could think about was how close Caleb was to her.

How it felt when his leg brushed hers.

And as she secretly glanced at him out of the corner of her eye, her heart beat just a bit faster and every word that came out of the speaker's mouth was like a muffled trombone inside her head.

All she could think of was Caleb saying it was a date.

What had she gotten herself into?

Hazel didn't know what she'd agreed to. She had, thankfully, packed one little black dress on the insistence of Bria, who'd warned her there might be a fancy dinner or a cocktail hour. Hazel had done away with her rainbow-colored socks and all the other clothes that made her feel comfortable.

What am I doing? she asked herself again as she looked in the full-length mirror. She didn't know how to answer that, but at least tonight she wouldn't be sitting in her hotel room alone.

Thinking about Caleb.

She grabbed her purse and a pashmina and headed down to the lobby. Caleb was there, waiting for her. He was wearing that same overcoat, the one he'd wrapped around her just before they had kissed at the falls.

And just thinking back to that moment made her swoon a bit. Though she had no right to swoon when she was feeling guilty about holding back something so important from him because of patient confidentiality.

She didn't like keeping secrets from anyone.

Especially from him.

He smiled when he saw her and it made her heart skip a beat.

"You look lovely, Hazel."

"Thanks." She was a lot a loss for words when he came closer.

He leaned over her and whispered against her ear. "I miss the rainbow socks though."

Heat unfurled in her belly as he placed a hand on the small of her back and they walked outside to a waiting cab. Her pulse was thundering between her ears, and she didn't know what to say as they sat in the back of the cab, his arm around her shoulders.

It was a short cab ride to the Space Needle, and they took the full elevator to the top and the rotating restaurant.

All she could do was focus on moving forward because her legs were shaking so bad it was hard to stay upright, especially in heels.

The maître d' led them to their table. The city of Seattle was lit up against the darkness. It was all twinkling lights and romantic music, and she couldn't hear anything but her heart beating erratically with her nerves.

Caleb pulled out a chair for her and she sat down. He handed his coat to the maître d' and she took in the sight of him in a well-tailored suit. It made her mouth water, thinking about what might lie underneath that expensive suit.

He took a seat across from her, tucking in his tie as he sat down. His gaze locked with hers across the table. "Are you quite all right?"

"What?" she asked.

"You seem distracted."

Hazel laughed nervously. "It's the lack of rainbow socks. They're the source of my superpowers, you know. So I guess I feel out of sorts without them."

He grinned. "I knew it."

"It's been a while since I've been out...like this. The last person who wined and dined me was my ex-boyfriend and even then it was all a show. I found out later that he'd had so many other girlfriends on the side. Although, I only ever caught him with one. That's what you get for trusting someone," she said a little bitterly.

"You can trust others," he said.

"Can I? I trusted him completely, and he broke my heart. I should've seen the signs."

"He sounds like a fool."

"Maybe I was the fool for being duped?" she said sardonically.

"Doubtful."

"Why doubtful?"

"He was a user. He took advantage of your caring nature. He's the vilest type of person."

A blush crept up her neck and she looked away. "Well, it's lovely to get out anyways."

"Agreed." They shared a brief smile. "It's been some time for me too, and it's apparently nice to do this or so I've been told."

"Who told you that?" Hazel asked.

"Lizzie, actually. 'Dad, people date all the time. Dinners out are nice,'" he teased.

"That's a smart girl you have there. How is she doing?"

He shot her a worried look. "So you've noticed her sickness as well?" he asked.

Her palms began to sweat again. Yes, she'd noticed her "illness." It was pregnancy, and apparently Lizzie still hadn't told her father yet. "Yes, she mentioned how stressed she was, and of course flu is going around at the moment."

She really hated lying to him.

Caleb frowned. He didn't look convinced.

"In any event she'd like to have you over for dinner again soon. She enjoyed your company very much."

"And did you?" she asked, her breath catching in her throat.

"I did as well. I do." He smiled, those blue-gray eyes twinkling in the dim light. "We don't have many people over. There's no one to invite."

"You don't have any extended family?" Hazel asked, trying to make conversation, even though she already knew the answer.

"No. As I said, my parents are both gone and I was an only child. My late wife had no family either. It was just us, and then it was me and Lizzie. It can get lonely sometimes."

"I'm sure. I have a large extended family, but we're spread out all over. It's hard to get together often. I miss them a lot."

"So you understand how isolating it can be," he stated.

"Yes," she agreed. She was lonely, but she put that out of her mind. She didn't like to think about it. Maybe she'd been so blind to Mark's cheating because she'd been lonely when she met him. He'd filled a hole in her heart.

Only she realized he hadn't.

Not really.

"I should have more people over," he groused. "When my wife died, I just focused on raising a baby and working. It was all I could do to get through the day, but I meant what I said... Lizzie wasn't the only one who enjoyed your company that evening. I did too. Immensely."

"Really?"

"It's nice having you around. You keep things... interesting."

She laughed. "Oh, dear, we do have our moments of not seeing eye to eye, don't we?"

"I'm telling you, it's the socks." His eyes twinkled in the dim light of the restaurant. "I enjoy your company, Hazel. I've missed you recently."

She wanted to tell him that she liked being around him too, but the waiter came and took their order. The conversation over dinner shifted to the lecture and discussion of Mrs. Patterson. They both agreed that Sandra, as long as she was stable, could stay at home. As long as she rested.

Sandra wanted a natural birth, if at all possible, but they would determine that next course of action when the babies were further along.

Hazel agreed the quints had to be delivered at St. Raymond's. It was clear to her they both wanted the best care for Sandra and the quints.

After they split the bill, they both decided to walk the short distance back to the hotel.

The night had cleared and the crisp air was lovely.

She shivered slightly.

"Are you cold?" he asked.

"Just a bit." What she didn't tell him was that she wanted him to wrap her up in his arms under that coat again.

What're you thinking?

She didn't know.

This was not keeping her distance from him at all, but also their conversation about loneliness had got to her. She'd forgotten how lonely she really was. He walked her to her room and they stood at her door, for what felt like an eternity.

The thing was, she didn't want him to go.

She didn't want this night to end.

"Thank you for inviting me out tonight," she said nervously.

"Thank you for agreeing to come with me. I was surprised to see you here."

"Same."

"It was a good surprise though," he admitted. "I didn't want to come here."

"Why?" she asked.

"I don't know," he said. "Work has been busy, and it seemed like a hassle."

"It's hard to get to these kinds of conventions."

"I texted you. You didn't respond."

Hazel bit her bottom lip. "I didn't get it. I thought…"

"Is this about the kiss again?" he asked, taking a step closer. "The one we didn't talk about."

"Yes."

"I scared you away?"

"No. It's just…" Only she couldn't think of the why she shouldn't pursue this. Even if just for one night. That logical part of her brain went quiet, and all she wanted to do was kiss him again.

So she did. Her body thrumming with anticipation as she pulled the lapels of his overcoat close and kissed him the way she'd been thinking about for so long. Only she didn't pull away afterward. Instead, she deepened the kiss, opening her mouth, their tongues entwining as she pressed her body against his.

"Hazel," he murmured against her neck as she slipped her arms around him inside his coat. "I want you. I think I've wanted you since the moment I met you."

"I thought you detested me?" she teased. "Especially after I was so mean to you at that tribunal."

"No, just myself for being such an ass to you and yet so attracted to you at the same time."

"I want you too. Even if it's just for tonight. I want you to know I don't need forever."

And she didn't. At least that's what she was telling herself.

There was a part of her that did, but that part of her was deathly afraid and remembered the hurt. It reminded her that forever was not an option for her.

How could she trust another man again?

She'd been blinded before.

She'd given her all to a man who'd callously thrown her love away. She was never going through that again.

Ever.

Even if forever was what she'd always wanted.

She could have tonight though, and maybe after tonight she could forget about how Caleb made her feel. She could get him out of her system and move forward with her career plans.

"Are you sure?" he asked hesitantly, confirming her fear that he might not really want her. That he would hurt her in the end, but she forced those thoughts away. It was all about being here in this moment.

She kissed him again and then opened the door to her hotel room, pulling him in. "I'm sure."

She was sure about him and tonight.

Tonight she wanted to not feel alone.

Caleb couldn't believe what was happening, and he was glad she wanted him as much as he wanted her. When she kissed him, it fired his blood. This was what he'd wanted ever since he met her. His blood was singing with want.

With need.

He wanted to touch her all over and have nothing between them.

Hazel pulled off his overcoat and then his suit jacket, kissing him and touching him. He ran his hands over her and unzipped her dress, marveling at the exquisite view of her in her lace underthings. Her long auburn hair fell down over her shoulders. As he ran his fingers through it, he discovered it was soft and silky, just like her skin. He ran his hand over her body, trailing his fingers over her flesh, leaving a trail of goose bumps in their wake.

She sighed.

It was too much to take in.

He was burning up.

"Hazel, I've dreamed about this for so long." He pressed a kiss against her neck, feeling her pulse fluttering under his lips.

"Same," she murmured, wrapping her arms around him.

Her hands undid his tie and shirt. They made quick work of the rest of their clothes. Except she left on her black stockings and high heels. He liked that.

She pulled him over to the bed beside her.

He reached for her, feeling her quiver under his touch. His hand moved between her legs, gently stroking her.

She moaned and moved her hips against his fingers. All he could think of was burying himself inside her. It was driving him crazy.

"What about protection?" he groaned. He didn't carry it because random sex was never his plan.

There was never time for trysts in hotel rooms. Until now.

The couple of times he had been with a woman had always been at her place, and she'd been prepared.

"It's okay. I carry some," she whispered. "I them to hand out in case they're needed by patients at the clinic."

She got the condom, opened it and before he could react she rolled it down his shaft. The touch made him burn even more. It was so simple, yet it drove him crazy with need.

He wanted her so bad.

He pressed her down and showed her how much

he wanted her. Kissing and licking her between her thighs.

Her hips moving against his mouth as he tasted her.

"Caleb," she murmured. "Please."

"What do you want?" he asked, though he knew because he wanted it too.

"Take me."

Caleb smiled and shifted his weight, teasing the folds of her sex with the tip of his shaft. She moved against him and he gritted his teeth, not wanting this to end. He thrust into her.

Sinking deeply.

Filling her completely.

"You feel so good," he moaned, and she did.

She was so soft, so wet and hot.

He was entirely lost to her.

"Oh, God," she murmured. Hazel met his slow thrusts, urging him to go faster until he complied. Soon, he couldn't hold back and he moved harder, faster, driven by a primal need to possess her completely.

He wanted this to last longer.

And he wanted her to come.

"Come for me, baby," he whispered against her neck.

She clutched his shoulders, her nails digging into his shoulder as she tightened around him, crying out as she came. He knew he was a lost man, and he came swiftly after her.

Melting in her exquisite heat.

When he floated down from heaven, he rolled over on his back and Hazel curled up beside him. He pulled her close, not wanting to let her go.

There was no need for words. He didn't even know what to say.

He was falling in love with her, and that was a terrifying prospect indeed.

CHAPTER NINE

HAZEL WOKE UP and gazed at Caleb sleeping soundly next to her. She smiled because his usually neat hair was curly and mussed.

It was all discombobulated because of what they'd been up to. They'd spent half the night in each other's arms. Hazel didn't know how good it could be with the right person. Being with Mark had been great, but last night with Caleb had been something she had never felt before.

It had consumed her.

And it had terrified her with how earth-shattering it had been.

It scared her how much she wanted more.

She'd been so sure one time with Caleb would be enough.

Now she wasn't.

Caleb wasn't looking for forever, which was apparent since he hadn't moved on after his wife died. And neither was she.

Aren't you?

She shook her head, trying to banish that niggly thought from her mind. Of course, it was hard not to let her walls down and think that way when she was with him, especially after last night.

He'd been that broody, stubborn, by the book doctor with an air of vulnerability, who'd always made her groan when she saw him. How could she be falling in love with him?

Why did she always seem to fall for the wrong kind of man?

Is Caleb the wrong kind of man though?

Her brain told her that he was, but her heart was saying that he was everything right. Her heart was convinced that Dr. Caleb Norris was everything she wanted in a man, but she just couldn't wrap her mind around that. Especially since she didn't really know how he felt about relationships, and she was still so wary of being hurt.

She rested her chin on her stacked fists watching him sleep.

A thrum of excitement coursed through her as she thought of his hands on her last night. The way his kisses had burned into her flesh, the pleasure that he'd made her feel. It had been a long time since she'd been intimate with a man, but she couldn't recall ever feeling that kind of heat or intensity with anyone else.

"I can feel you watching me," Caleb murmured without opening his eyes. "Why? Are you plotting my demise? Was this your goal all along?"

She laughed softly. "I'm not plotting anything. I'm discreetly trying to make a dignified exit, and I got caught up in your cuteness."

"Cuteness? I'm hardly young enough to be considered cute," he said, quirking an eyebrow but still not opening his eyes. "Why are you trying to leave? The bed is so warm and comfy."

"My flight back to Portland is in three hours."

He opened his eyes and glanced at the time. "Damn. I meant to text Lizzie last night."

He jumped up, and she admired his bottom as he searched for his trousers in their tangled pile of clothing. He dug out his phone and frowned. "I turned the ringer off for the lecture. Blast."

"What's wrong?" she asked, her stomach sinking.

"No text from Lizzie, but missed calls and pages from Dr. Victor Anderson at St. Raymond's. He's the chief of staff there."

"Yes. I know. I've met Victor," Hazel replied. What she didn't say was that Victor had been the first person she and Bria had met. The one who'd welcomed the idea of their birthing center with open arms. "You better call."

Caleb nodded and called Victor back. She grabbed her phone and saw Lizzie had texted her.

The texts were frantic.

Lizzie was in pain and needed help but was alone. Something about feeling shoulder pain. More like agony.

Hazel's heart stopped for a moment, and a lump formed in her throat as she stared at the texts.

"Hi, Victor. It's Caleb. I forgot to turn my ringer back on."

Caleb's face drained of color as he listened.

"When? Right. What's wrong? Okay. I'll be there as soon as I can. What? Okay great. I'm on my way."

He ended the call and ran his hand through his hair, looking frantic.

"Lizzie texted me," Hazel said. "She was in panic. In pain."

"Yes. She collapsed, and her boyfriend took her to St. Raymond's last night. Victor said they've sedated her and did an MRI. They suspect an ectopic pregnancy."

He didn't look at her.

"I couldn't tell you. She had to tell you herself. She's an adult," Hazel stated. She hated that Lizzie's secret had finally come out this way. She'd known that she couldn't tell him, and it broke her a bit that Caleb wasn't looking at her now.

He, of all people, should understand patient confidentiality, but it was obvious he was hurt that she couldn't tell him about Lizzie. Just like it had pained her to keep it from him.

Caleb didn't respond. "I have to get back. The fallopian tube could rupture. I have to be there."

"Oh, Caleb," Hazel said softly. Her heart was sinking for Lizzie, so alone and afraid.

"Dr. Anderson has arranged for a helicopter flight back to Portland. Lizzie wants you there as her midwife. Since you diagnosed her pregnancy."

It was the way he said that last part that caused a shudder to go through her.

Almost like he was blaming her, but she wanted to give him the benefit of the doubt.

He was worried about his daughter, that was all.

"I'll come to Portland."

"Thank you," he said curtly as he pulled on his clothes. "I'll go pack, and I'll meet you downstairs in twenty minutes."

"Yes."

He left her room and her heart was still in her throat.

Other than Lizzie's illness, there had been no other signs of ectopic pregnancy.

Except her extreme feelings of sickness, but that could be present in any pregnancy and her HCG levels had been consistent. Sometimes with an ectopic, they weren't as high.

She felt like the she was at fault. Only, she wasn't. An MRI could pick up the ectopic pregnancy. She couldn't by examination alone. But all she knew now was that she wanted to help Lizzie any way she could.

If it wasn't dealt with right away the tube could rupture, as Caleb had mentioned, and if it did that she'd bleed to death.

It broke her heart that there was no saving the baby because she knew Lizzie had wanted it, even though she was so young, but most likely the baby was gone. They usually were at this point.

Hazel got dressed as fast as she could. A shower could wait until they got to Portland.

After she was dressed and packed, she headed to the lobby and checked out. Caleb was already waiting and pacing by the main door.

"You ready?" he asked abruptly.

"Yes. Let's go."

Caleb hailed a cab.

It was a short ride to the private airfield just outside of Seattle, and it helped that it was a Sunday morning. Traffic was minimal. The helicopter was being primed and ready for them. All Hazel could think about was Lizzie and getting home to her safely.

She could tell that was on Caleb's mind too.

They were given headphones to muffle the sounds of the chopper, and it wasn't long before the aircraft took off, flying away from Seattle down toward Portland.

Hazel reached out and took his hand in hers. Caleb looked down but didn't smile, and instead of accepting the gesture he pulled his hand away. It stung. It wasn't her fault she couldn't tell him about Lizzie. He knew why she hadn't, yet he was still blaming her.

And it broke her heart even more.

Why did she let herself fall for Caleb? She knew better than this.

"Thank you again for coming at Lizzie's request," he said mechanically over the microphone.

"Where else would I be?"

He didn't say anything else, but she could tell he was both mad and worried.

It was like a slap in the face. After their night together, somehow she was taking the brunt of his shock over learning Lizzie was pregnant and the terror that he might lose his child. That he was able to push her aside so easily after their night together really hurt, but she understood all the same.

That's what you wanted, isn't it? For him to keep his distance from you?

Except she wasn't so sure about that now, and she was scared. She'd risked her heart once again, against her own better judgment, and got burned.

She was utterly crushed.

The helicopter ride took a couple of hours, and it landed on the roof of St. Raymond's. They headed down to the surgical unit.

Dr. Anderson was waiting there when they got to Lizzie's room, as was Dr. Gracie, Caleb's OB/ GYN fellow.

"How is she?" Caleb asked.

"Stable and we gave her some pain medication. As Victor told you, we did an MRI and the fallopian tube has not ruptured yet. We need to get her into surgery," Dr. Gracie said.

"Fine. I'll go get prepped…" Caleb started.

Victor shook his head. "You're her father. You can't. She did ask for Ms. Rees though."

Caleb was going to argue, but closed his mouth.

"Then I want Hazel in there with her, since that's what Lizzie wants."

Dr. Gracie looked confused. "The midwife?"

"Yes, I'm Lizzie's midwife," Hazel replied firmly. "I'm also a nurse practitioner."

Dr. Gracie didn't look that impressed. "Fine. She can be in the operating room."

Lizzie was her patient, and she was going to advocate for her.

"I'd like to see the MRI," Caleb said.

"I figured." Victor brought up the MRI on a tablet. "You can see the mass here in the fallopian tube. It's a nonviable pregnancy."

Caleb's lips pursed in a thin line. "When is the surgery scheduled?" he asked quietly.

"As soon as possible now that you're here," Victor responded. "Right, Dr. Gracie?"

Dr. Gracie nodded. "The operating room is being prepped as we speak."

"Well, I'll sign the forms, since I'm her next of kin and she's sedated, and let's get her into surgery," Caleb stated.

"Timothy won't be happy Ms. Rees is in there," Dr. Gracie said.

Caleb frowned. "I don't care. Hazel is Lizzie's midwife. She diagnosed Lizzie's pregnancy. Lizzie trusts her. If I can't be there, Hazel will be."

Dr. Gracie nodded stiffly. "Very well. Ms. Rees, I'll show you where to get scrubs."

Caleb went into Lizzie's room and sat next to her

bed. Hazel's heart hurt seeing him so distraught, but she was going to make sure that Lizzie was taken care of. She may not be welcome in the hospital and Caleb might not be very happy with her right now, but that didn't matter.

She was still Lizzie's midwife.

Maybe even a friend?

She was a trained medical professional, and she belonged here.

Dr. Gracie showed her into the staff locker room and handed her scrubs. "We do respect patient wishes here, Ms. Rees. I'm not against you or your center."

"I get it. Your board of directors is. I'm familiar with the politics of the hospital."

"Are you?" he asked stiffly.

"I worked at a hospital as a midwife and as a nurse practitioner. I know how they work."

"I'm glad you understand," Dr. Gracie said. "I'll meet you at Lizzie's room, and we'll take her down to the operating room."

She had a feeling he wasn't particularly glad though.

Hazel nodded. She put her suitcase in a locker and got changed.

Lizzie looked so small lying sedated in her bed. She was so much like Jane, with her long blond hair fanned out across the pillows. The only difference was that Lizzie had a purple streak in her hair.

Purple streak? When did she get that? Why hadn't he protected her better? Why couldn't he have stopped this?

He would've noticed her pregnancy sooner if he hadn't been so obsessed lately with Hazel.

He was the worst father.

He could've stopped her from seeing that boy, and Caleb was about ready to throttle Derek for getting his daughter pregnant when they were still in college.

Lizzie is an adult now, remember? And it takes two to tango.

Caleb sighed and sat down in the chair by her bedside.

He'd promised Jane that he would take care of Lizzie. They'd had that talk when she was pregnant, that if anything happened to either of them, the other one would always put Lizzie first.

He'd thought he was doing that, but how did he miss this?

Because you've been preoccupied for too long.

He'd basically just concentrated on getting through each day ever since Jane died. He'd thought work would help keep the pain away. Hold back all that grief, but really it had been numbing him to life.

He'd been missing things for years.

Important things like this.

Lizzie was sick and he'd thought it was the flu.

Now, looking back, he could see the pregnancy signs. He hadn't seen anything at the time, and now this was all his fault.

He was so selfish.

"Caleb, it's time."

Caleb turned to see Hazel in dark blue scrubs, her hair tied back and covered by a scrub cap. He barely recognized her.

Hazel had lied to him.

She'd known for weeks that Lizzie was pregnant and didn't tell him.

He felt betrayed, hurt that Hazel had kept from him what was going on with his daughter. Did she know it was an ectopic pregnancy?

Did she do all the right exams?

He was questioning everything and he wasn't sure what to believe, but none of that mattered right now. All that mattered was Lizzie.

"Take care of her," he said, hoping his voice didn't shake.

"Of course," Hazel said gently as the porters came in to wheel Lizzie's bed away.

Caleb took a step back and watched his daughter go, feeling completely helpless and powerless.

It was an ectopic pregnancy.

That could've been his grandchild. Now it was putting his only child's life at risk.

She could die on the operating table. Just like Jane had.

Don't think like that.
Lizzie was going to be okay.
She had to be okay.

CHAPTER TEN

HAZEL SCRUBBED IN. She stared through the window that separated the scrub area from the operating room, which was in front of her. It wasn't one of the main rooms, but one that was used for day procedures. It had been some time since she'd attended a surgery. When she had been in nursing school, she had done several surgical rotations.

It wasn't her favorite place to be, but Lizzie wanted her here so this is where she'd be.

Lizzie had been transferred to the surgical table and was being prepped for the surgery. Depending on the damage, they might be able to save her fallopian tube.

Dr. Gracie had scrubbed in and was standing next to the bed as the equipment for the surgery was laid out and set up by the scrub nurse.

As she looked at a fully functioning and state-of-the-art operating room, a shudder ran down her spine. Not because of the sterile environment, but because Lizzie was going to be here on the operating table.

Exposed.

At the mercy of the surgeon.

A lump formed in her throat. This was the part of obstetrics she hated.

The loss of life.

Except it would kill Lizzie if her body tried to hold on to a baby that wasn't viable. And her life, here, was the most important.

She hated seeing Lizzie on the table.

Hazel toweled off and stepped into the operating room. A nurse helped her into a gown and gloves.

Dr. Gracie looked up. "Are you ready, Ms. Rees?"

"Yes. I'm ready." Hazel glanced down at Lizzie and swallowed the lump that had formed in her throat. She cared about Lizzie, just like she cared about Caleb, and there was a part of her that wanted to be part of their little family. But Caleb blamed her for Lizzie's situation, so the chances of that dream ever happening were slim indeed.

She put those thoughts out of her mind and took her place by Lizzie's side. Although the young woman was sedated and unaware, Hazel was here for her.

This was where she needed to be.

"Okay, let's get started," Dr. Gracie announced. "Scalpel."

The instrument was handed over.

"Ovary and mass located," Dr. Gracie said once Lizzie was opened up. "Making an incision."

Hazel watched the monitor with bated breath as Dr. Gracie removed the nonviable pregnancy. The tube was pretty scarred, so he had to remove the damaged portion of the fallopian tube and seal it.

She tried not to watch the clock as the procedure went on.

"Ready to close," Dr. Gracie finally said. "She should make a full recovery."

Hazel checked Lizzie and saw that everything looked stable, for now. Dr. Gracie placed a dressing over the incision.

The nurses took Lizzie out of the operating room to wheel her back to her room.

Hazel pulled off her surgical gown and scrubbed out. She hoped the lab results wouldn't take long. She wandered out of the scrub room and made her way back to the staff room to change.

As she walked along the hallway, she ran smack-dab into Dan Patterson.

"Mr. Patterson?" Hazel asked, shocked.

"Hazel, I didn't expect to see you. They said you don't work here."

"I don't…is everything okay with Sandra?" Hazel asked.

"So far. We came in for an ultrasound on Friday, and she was admitted. We wanted you paged, but I'm not sure they did."

"Sandra was admitted? Do you know why?"

Dan shrugged. "Yeah, on Friday. We're here waiting for Dr. Norris to tell us why."

"Dr. Norris?" Hazel asked.

"Yeah. We didn't see him, but the fellow who saw us on Friday said that our care was moving from the Multnomah Falls Women's Health Center to St. Raymond's per Dr. Norris's orders. We didn't question it because you referred him to us in the first place."

"Of course. You're right, I did."

"Sorry, Hazel. We would rather be at home or your center, but if it means the babies and my wife are safe, then we have to stay here."

"Absolutely," Hazel said in shock. Dan headed back to his wife's room. Hazel stood there, in hospital scrubs, stunned. She felt like she'd been betrayed. Why had she let down her walls? Why had she trusted Caleb?

And just like Mark, Caleb had obviously lied to her. He hadn't told her that she'd been removed from the case, but he must have known. It was what Timothy Russell and the board of directors had wanted right from the start.

Only, she'd thought Caleb was on her side. Why hadn't he fought to keep her on the case, where she belonged?

Dr. Gracie had said Timothy wouldn't be happy she was here, and Caleb had promised that he would make sure she was. That she would stay as the main practitioner on Sandra's case. She felt like she had been kicked in the gut. She'd thought she and Caleb were colleagues.

Friends.

No, she'd thought they were something even more.

She'd trusted him.

Once again she'd been betrayed by a man she'd come to care for, and she was angry at herself for trusting him.

For falling for him.

Her walls were there for a good reason. Why had she forgotten that?

Because you fell in love with the wrong person. Again.

Tears stung her eyes and she quickly wiped them away. She was a fool. She was going to rebuild her walls, stronger this time, and she was never going to let them down ever again.

Lizzie was still a bit groggy as she started to wake up.

"Dad?" she asked.

"I'm here," Caleb said, gently stroking her face. "I'm right here."

"Is Hazel here? I texted her…"

"Yes," Caleb said. "She was in Seattle at the same lecture as me."

Lizzie nodded. "I like her."

Caleb smiled a little stiffly. "I like her too. She's a good…midwife."

He was still hurt Hazel had kept him in the dark about his daughter, but that didn't detract from Hazel's talent.

Lizzie wrinkled her nose. "Come on…"

"What?"

Lizzie shook her head and didn't answer. "What's wrong with me?"

He wanted to tell her that the baby was gone, that she'd lost one of her fallopian tubes, but she was still coming out of anesthetic.

He didn't even know how Lizzie had felt about the baby. He wasn't sure how he was feeling now. All he knew was Lizzie had come through the surgery successfully.

She was alive.

That was all that mattered to him.

Lizzie drifted off to sleep again, and he scrubbed a hand over his face. Not sure of what to think.

Hazel knocked on the door. Instantly he noticed something was off about, her and it sent a shiver of dread down his spine. Had something happened during the surgery he didn't know about?

She seemed tense.

"How is she doing?" Hazel asked, her arms folded across her chest.

"Groggy. I'll tell her what's happened when she's more alert."

Hazel smiled slightly, but he knew something was wrong with her. The smile didn't reach her eyes the way it had done just last night.

It was like a wall had been put up between them again. Like when they had been standing in the elevator in Seattle. She was suddenly shutting him out.

Not that he could blame her.

He was still annoyed that she'd known about Lizzie, but said nothing. Especially with his daughter's life on the line like that.

He'd been thinking so much about Hazel, he hadn't seen Lizzie's pregnancy signs for what they were.

"Hazel?" Lizzie asked groggily.

"I'm here," Hazel said gently, coming closer to the bed.

Lizzie smiled. "I'm glad you're here."

"Of course, where else would I be?" Hazel responded, touching Lizzie's shoulder gently.

Lizzie just nodded and drifted back off again.

Hazel smiled at her fondly and then looked up at him. The smile that was in her eyes for Lizzie fizzled out when their gazes locked. Red bloomed in her cheeks.

"I've got to go," she said quickly.

"Hazel, what aren't you telling me? Did something bad happen during the surgery?"

"The surgery went off without a hitch. Nothing unexpected happened." Hazel walked out of the room, and Caleb followed her into the hall. He closed the door to Lizzie's room.

"Hazel."

"Now you want to talk?" she asked bitterly.

"What's that supposed to mean?"

"You were pretty curt to me on the way back to Portland."

"I was worried about Lizzie."

"So was I." She turned to leave.

"Hazel!"

She turned around, seemingly annoyed with him. "What, Caleb?"

"What's wrong?"

"I ran into Dan Patterson after the surgery."

Caleb was confused. "I don't understand."

"He told me that Sandra was admitted, and they don't know why. And they tried to page me, but that under your orders I've been removed as her practitioner."

"She was having contractions during a routine ultrasound. My fellow called me, and it was only right to admit her until the results of her other tests came through."

Hazel nodded. "Okay, then why was I removed as one of her health care providers?"

"What?" Caleb asked, stunned.

"I have been removed as one of the Pattersons' health care providers. You're their primary doctor now."

"I will correct it," Caleb stated.

"Don't bother. It's what you wanted from the get-go. It was evident when you didn't stand up for me with Timothy Russell after Mrs. Jameson's VBAC."

"What are you talking about?"

"Since the moment we met you've been trying to shut down our center and get me to leave. Why not take my patients too?"

"That wasn't me," he said hotly. "You know that. You're letting your temper get the better of you."

"Why? Why did you take me off the Pattersons'

case? I thought you at least respected me professionally. I thought—"

"I do," Caleb snapped. "And you thought what?"

He was hurt that she thought he could be this cruel. He was going to find out why she was removed from the case, but he wanted her to understand that it wasn't his fault. He wanted her to believe him. If she cared about him at all, she would understand what he was trying to say, but she hadn't been up front with him either. She hadn't let him know what was going on with Lizzie.

"No. You don't and it's nothing. It doesn't matter what I think."

Caleb took a step closer. "It does matter. Why aren't you listening to what I'm saying? Why are you throwing up walls again? Why do you keep shutting me out?"

"I'm not shutting you out and you're one to talk. You've been doing it since your wife died. Isolating yourself."

It was like a slap in the face, but it was true. Why couldn't she see that he wasn't like that with her? Why was she being so obtuse about this?

"You're pushing me away. You can trust me," Caleb said.

"Can I?" she asked, glowering at him.

Caleb crossed his arms. "Hazel, I don't fully understand what is happening here."

"I've been betrayed before. You know that. You know I've been used and hurt before. You got so close to me, slept with me and while my back was turned you undermined me."

"I didn't undermine you! And I'm not trying to hurt you. You're the one with the walls firmly up. You're pushing me away now to protect yourself. And don't forget, I'm not the only one withholding information, am I?"

He knew this was going to happen. He'd put his heart on the line, and here he was getting hurt again. He couldn't think straight.

She looked stung. "I couldn't say anything about Lizzie's pregnancy. She's eighteen. I had to abide by patient confidentiality. You're using that as an excuse to have a go at me, and you're being totally unfair. You would've done the same thing if our situations were reversed, and don't deny it. It killed me that I couldn't tell you what was happening. I hate deceit and you know why."

"But I could've lost Lizzie. She's all I have! You have no idea how that feels. You have no one." He regretted what he said the moment he said it, but he was too angry and scared.

Right now, he felt like his world was spinning out of control. He hated this loss of control.

"Caleb…"

"Don't," he said quickly.

"I'll let you have some time to yourself," Hazel said. "It's clear neither of us is ready for anything more."

He could hear the sadness in her voice, and he felt the pain his heart.

Maybe she was right.

So he let her walk away.

And he was left with just his own thoughts.

Today had started so perfectly. He had woken up next to Hazel after an amazing night in her arms. He'd foolishly opened his heart to her, and she'd pushed him away. Now, his daughter had lost her baby, and he hadn't even known what danger signs to look out for because he hadn't known about the pregnancy.

How was he going to tell Lizzie? He didn't know.

He was alone, and right now he needed a friend, except the friend he'd had, the woman he'd loved, didn't want him. There was no point in denying it. He'd fallen in love with Hazel. It had been so long since he had felt this way, he'd almost not recognized it.

He never thought he'd feel love again.

He'd ruined his chance with her. He'd accused her of lying to him in the heat of his despair over Lizzie. But he could see that, really, she'd had no other choice.

She was right. If the situations were reversed, he would've done the same. He couldn't have told her.

But there was no trust between them. How could they move forward without that essential building block of any relationship?

Hazel didn't believe him about not being in-

volved in taking away her case. He was angry at
Timothy for that, but he was sad Hazel couldn't
trust him.

Wouldn't trust him.

Hazel's heart was breaking, and she had a hard
time holding back the tears that were threatening
to spill over.

Why?

Why did she have to fall in love with him?

It was clear he didn't want a relationship with
her. Now she had to work with him while trying to
repress her feelings. It was going to be a nightmare.

She was not going to hide. She had important
work to do at the birthing center, and although it
would still be hard to see him, she'd have to sometimes. She wiped away the tears on the back of
her hand.

Hazel went into Lizzie's room to check on her.

Lizzie woke up when Hazel shut the door to her
room. "Hazel?"

"Yes." She walked over to the bed and sat down
on the edge.

"What is it?" Lizzie asked.

Hazel sighed, trying to make sure that she could
control all the emotions going through her. "Lizzie,
your pregnancy was ectopic."

"What?"

"It means your baby grew outside of the uterus.

AMY RUTTAN

In your fallopian tube. It wasn't viable and your tube was so scarred. We couldn't save it."

Lizzie paled. "My baby is gone?"

"Yes. I'm so sorry," Hazel said, fighting back tears.

Lizzie nodded. "Does my dad know?"

"Yes. They had to tell him. You were sedated. Your life was in danger."

Lizzie frowned. "I didn't want him to worry. It's why I could never tell him. I tried several times, believe me. He always worries, and he'd been so happy lately with you around. So I just kept my pain to myself. I knew he'd be so disappointed in me. I couldn't bear it. I did try and tell him. I swear."

"I was going to talk to you about telling him," Hazel said.

Lizzie nodded, breaking into sobs. "I know. I wanted to, but I just couldn't."

Hazel's heart broke, and she fought to regain her composure. Lizzie had tried to do what was best for her dad, but that hadn't worked out and it hurt her that Lizzie had only wanted her dad to be happy with her.

"He will always worry about you, because he's your father. It's kind of the job," Hazel said, clearing her throat.

"Yes, but he's had no life because of me. He raised me all on his own."

"It's not because of you." Although, Hazel didn't

really know why Caleb didn't date or socialize more. He just seemed to work.

As do you. So why don't you date?

Hazel shook that niggly logical thought away. "Lizzie, you need to talk to him. You need to tell him everything. How you felt about the baby. How much you love Derek. I know you didn't want to tell him to protect him and not raise his stress levels, but he deserves to know."

Lizzie nodded. "Okay. I'll talk with him, but what if he doesn't…what if…"

Hazel pulled a trembling Lizzie into her arms. "He loves you. He won't ever disown you. It'll be okay. After all, you're here, aren't you? You survived the surgery. And you can still have babies. One day, when it's the right time for you."

Lizzie nodded and lay back down. "Okay. Can you get my dad?"

"Sure."

Hazel got up and left Lizzie's room.

Caleb was pacing. He was still processing everything.

Lizzie's pregnancy, the fact she'd hid it from him, that she'd felt the need to.

His fight with Hazel.

He'd messed so many things up.

Hazel came out of Lizzie's room. Her face stained with tears. Seeing her so broken up about his daughter melted his heart.

"I told her about the baby. She's an adult, and I'm her health care practitioner. I had to let her know."

"I understand," he said. And he did. It was her duty to tell Lizzie.

"Lizzie needs to speak with you."

Caleb nodded.

Lizzie was sitting up and looking worried. He could see she had been crying too.

Caleb walked into the room and Lizzie looked at him, wringing her hands.

"Dad." Her voice caught in her throat.

"I'm here." He went to her side and stroked her hair.

"Are you mad?"

"No."

"So you're not mad that I...?" Her lips began to tremble.

Caleb choked back his pain. "No. And I wouldn't have been even had I known. Why didn't you tell me?"

Tears slid down her face. "I didn't want to stress you out."

"You kept something so important from me because you were worried about stressing me out?"

Lizzie sighed. "You take such good care of me, Dad. I just didn't want you to worry. You've spent my whole life worrying. I'm an adult now. I want you to be free."

Caleb pulled Lizzie into his arms. "Worrying about you is my job. Whether you're an adult or not."

Lizzie cried on his shoulders. "Dad, I worry about you too."

"That's not your job," he said gently. "Your job is to get healthy."

"It's just the two of us though."

"I know."

"Dad, I really want you to be happy, and you've been so happy recently with Hazel."

His heart skipped a beat. He had been, but he had been trying to hold it back. "I want you to be happy too, Lizzie."

Lizzie nodded. "Derek and I want to get married after college."

"Okay."

Lizzie took a deep breath. "I know you wanted us to take it slow, because you and Mom were so young…"

"We were, but I was in love with her, and I don't regret ever having you or marrying your mom."

"It's going to crush Derek about the baby."

"Of course it will. I'm crushed too." He smoothed back her hair. "It's a part of life, sadly. He'll be happy you're safe and well though. I know I am."

Lizzie broke down crying again, and he held her in his arms. "I love you, Lizzie. So please don't worry and don't hide anything else from me."

"I won't, Dad, but I need you to be happy too. I mean Hazel…"

"She has her own life," Caleb said quickly. "Don't worry about me. Right now we have to focus on getting you better. I can't lose you, Lizzie. I promised your mother I would take care of you."

Lizzie gasped. "I promised her too, Dad. In my dreams. When I was a kid."

Caleb's eyes filled with tears. "You did?"

Lizzie nodded. "She wants you to be happy too and to let her go."

Caleb didn't know what to say. He just held his daughter until there was a knock at the door. Hazel stuck her head in, and his heart skipped a beat seeing her.

"Is everything okay?" Caleb asked, not sure he wanted to let his daughter go.

"No. It's Mrs. Patterson. I'm afraid they need you."

Caleb looked at Lizzie.

"Go, Dad. I've got the television and my phone. I'm fine."

Caleb kissed her on the forehead and followed Hazel out.

"What's happened?" he asked.

"They wouldn't tell me. I'm not on the case, remember," she said quickly.

"Yes, you are."

"What're you talking about?"

"I'm putting you on the case. I'm head of obstetrics, I'll petition the hospital board, and if they try to stop me from doing it, I'll leave. After we take care of Mrs. Patterson of course."

Hazel was stunned. "Thank you."

"It's the least I could do."

Only he could do more. He could apologize and make things right. Repair the trust between them. He could finally stop being such a fool and tell her how he really felt. Only he couldn't find the words in that moment, and there was no time right now.

Right now, he had several lives to save.

CHAPTER ELEVEN

CALEB GOT CHANGED into some scrubs and headed into Mrs. Patterson's room, with Hazel close on his heels. His fellow, Dr. Gracie, who'd admitted Mrs. Patterson when Caleb had been traveling to Seattle, was also there.

Mrs. Patterson was being comforted by her husband, and looked in distress.

"Dr. Gracie?" Caleb asked, taking the chart. Hazel looked over his shoulder to read all the labs and the information that had been collected since Sandra had been admitted.

Including the blatant removal of Hazel by the chairman of the board, which was not Caleb's wish at all. Her eyes widened and she blushed. He knew then that she'd spotted it wasn't him. It was Timothy all along.

"Patient is having signs of labor and upon examination there's a shortening of her cervix," Dr. Gracie remarked.

"Signs of labor?" Hazel asked, crossing her arms. "What kind of signs?"

Dr. Gracie barely glanced at Hazel. "Back pain, contractions. They're intermittent though."

"Thank you, Dr. Gracie," Caleb said. "Hazel Rees is going to assist. Can you check up on the post-op patients for me?"

Dr. Gracie was shocked, but didn't argue and left the room.

"What's wrong?" Sandra asked. Dan was holding her hand, and they both looked frightened.

"You're having some small, very irregular contractions and we're going to find out why," Caleb said. "Hazel, I'm sure you're familiar with cervical cerclage?"

"Yes," Hazel stated.

"Well, as Mrs. Patterson's practitioner, would you be the one to check?"

Hazel's eyes widened. "Of course."

Caleb stepped back and let Hazel sit down as he eyed the monitors.

"This is going to be cold, Sandra. I'm going to use the speculum," Hazel said as she prepared Sandra for the insertion.

Mrs. Patterson nodded and winced. "Okay, I'm ready."

"Just some pressure," Hazel said reassuringly.

Caleb peered over Hazel's shoulder and could see the cervix shortening. He and Hazel exchanged a knowing look. They both knew in that instant that Mrs. Patterson needed to have the cerclage to prevent preterm labor.

"Sandra, we're going to get anesthesiology in here and give you a spinal epidural before we put a tiny stitch in your cervix. That stitch should stop the shortening of your cervix and prevent you from going into labor or miscarrying," Hazel said. "Do you consent to this procedure?"

"Absolutely," Sandra said, her voice shaking. "I thought I could go home today, but do whatever you have to, to save my babies."

"When will it be taken out?" Dan asked.

"Usually by the thirty-seventh week. By then it's safe to deliver the babies. If labor starts and we're past thirty, at the minimum, we'll just remove it. Ideally I would like you to get to thirty-seven weeks," Caleb said. "Which will be a challenge. In your case, anything past thirty weeks is good enough when it comes to quints."

Hazel glanced at Caleb, and he felt bad that he wasn't here when Sandra was admitted by his fellow. He was also furious that he hadn't been here when Timothy had removed Hazel as main practitioner.

Dr. Gracie was young and did what he was told.

He'd been that way once too.

This whole thing was a mess and frankly, Caleb felt, it had made the hospital look bad. It wasn't a horrible hospital by any means, but the way the board was currently running things, it was a disgrace and would have a bad reputation soon enough.

"You're going to have to rest here for a couple more days and then, if you're stable, you can return home," Caleb said. "There is no reason to keep you here if everything looks fine."

Hazel removed the speculum and took off her gloves. "All good."

"I'll put in a call for anesthesiology," Caleb said. "Right now your contractions have ended, but we need to get this procedure done. I'll have an anesthesiologist come to do your spinal, and then we'll take you to the operating room."

"Okay," Sandra said. "Thank you, Hazel, Dr. Norris."

Caleb left. He had to get an operating room prepped.

And then there was Lizzie, who was mourning her own loss.

Caleb knew something about that, and he wanted to be there to help her through it.

Then there was Hazel.

They both had trust bridges to rebuild, and he wanted to do that. He wanted to make things right again. He just wasn't sure how best to go about it.

Caleb scrubbed a hand over his face.

He went to the nurses' station and made the appropriate arrangements for the cervical cerclage. After he made sure that anesthesiology was on their way, Hazel came out of Sandra's room and approached him at the nurses' station where he was trying to focus on the paperwork and not think about everything on his mind. He had to concentrate on his patient.

He just had to get through this surgery, and then

he wasn't sure what was going to happen next. He was incredibly frustrated with the board of directors at this hospital. Maybe it was time to open his own practice and not worry anymore about how this hospital was running.

There was a part of him, a long time ago, that had thought he might become a chief of staff at a place like this one day, but with all the political nonsense he'd seen here, he didn't want that now.

He could see the pressure that Victor was under. And how he kept an upbeat attitude about it was commendable.

Now he understood Hazel a bit better, why she'd pursued something that she was so passionate about and why she'd fought so hard for what she believed in.

Hazel was filling in some paperwork herself, so that she could officially have operating room privileges and access to everything she needed. Midwives shouldn't be treated like this. This hospital should be open and accepting of them.

He admired Hazel all the more for doing what she believed in.

He was completely in love with her.

He was going to make everything right. Even if she still didn't want him, he wasn't going to regret their night together. He was going to take a chance.

At least then he would know.

He was so tired of being alone and protecting his heart.

Life meant pain sometimes, and he was willing to risk that again if it meant that he could have Hazel. As long as he hadn't completely blown his chance with her by accusing her of things that weren't her fault and breaking her fragile trust in him.

He was finally willing to embrace the thing that scared him the most, and that was opening his heart back up to the possibility of love.

Hazel was back in the operating room. Sandra Patterson had taken her spinal epidural well and was awake on the surgical table. The scrub nurses were draping her, and Caleb was prepping what would be needed for the cervical cerclage.

Dan was sitting on the opposite side of the drape and comforting his wife. Right up to the last moment, Hazel wasn't sure if she would be allowed in here, because the hospital had been so hell-bent on making sure that she didn't have privileges.

She'd seen from the file it wasn't Caleb who'd taken her off the case, and she had been foolish to jump the gun and blame him. She had been so hurt before by a man that she loved, Hazel had expected Caleb to do the same.

She'd thought Caleb was different, but he had badly hurt her when he'd blamed her for not telling him about Lizzie's pregnancy.

You know he was just scared for his child.

She might not know how he felt in that situation, but she understood it. She cared for Lizzie too.

Being in that operating room, watching Lizzie have surgery, had terrified her.

Caleb hadn't cheated on her or lied to her. She had lashed out at him before she knew the whole truth about why she'd been removed from the case. It was that fiery temper of hers again. She needed to find Caleb and have a calm discussion so they could sort this whole mess out. She had to stop pushing him away.

Not that it took much. She'd known all along that he wasn't ready to open his heart again. He had a lot on his plate. And even more now with Lizzie healing from surgery and loss.

A lump caught in her throat as she finished scrubbing up.

Hazel was absolutely exhausted, but she was going to be there for that young woman. She wished she could be there for her more.

She longed to be a part of Caleb and Lizzie's family.

But if Caleb wasn't ready that was fine.

If Caleb was too hurt because he felt she had let him down by not telling him about Lizzie's baby, then that was fine. They could still be friends. They could still be colleagues. Even if St. Raymond's was still going to give her a hard time about com-

ing to work here, at least she would have an advocate on the other side. Caleb would make sure that
she got access if her patients needed it.

She only hoped that the same courtesy would be
extended to Bria.

Hazel finished her scrubbing in. She shook off
her hands and dried them with a paper towel, slip-
ping on her mask and then stepping into the operating room. A nurse helped her on with a gown
and a surgical shield with light.

Sandra looked in her direction as she walked toward the surgical table.

"Hazel, am I going to be okay?" Sandra asked,
her voice shaking.

"Yes. This is done all the time," Hazel said gently. "You won't feel a thing and neither will the babies. I promise."

Sandra nodded. "Thank you, Hazel. I'm so glad
you're back on my case. I'd go elsewhere to have
you."

"I'm glad too." Hazel made her way down to the
end of the surgical table. Mrs. Patterson's legs were
placed in the stirrups, and Hazel sat down on the
rolling chair. Caleb sat next to her.

They didn't have to say anything. Caleb was
there to hand her what she needed. Hazel made
sure that Mrs. Patterson was numb and went to
work. It was a simple procedure, and she had done
this on her midwife patients before.

It was nice working with Caleb beside her.

She finished the stitch and everything looked good.

"I'm all done, Sandra!" Hazel finished and removed the speculum. "We're going to move you to post-op, and it can take some time before the effects of the spinal wear off."

Sandra nodded. "Everything is okay?"

"Yes. I don't see any complications. I will check on you later."

"Thank you, Hazel and Dr. Norris," Sandra said.

Hazel nodded and left the operating room and headed back to the scrub room. Caleb followed her and started scrubbing out as well.

"I got a page from Victor while you were doing the cerclage," Caleb said, not looking at her.

"Oh?"

"Besides Timothy being livid, Victor wanted me to tell you that the staff of St. Raymond's are behind you."

"Are they?" she asked in surprise.

"Yes. I am too. The rest of the board now knows the Pattersons will leave if you're not on the case."

"What about you?"

He shrugged. "That doesn't matter. They came to you first. Besides, I have a lot to think about and Lizzie to take care of."

"She'll be okay, Caleb."

He smiled at her. "I know. I can't lose her. I'm tired of losing the people I love."

He left her standing there.

Did he love her?

Is that what he was implying? Then she shook her head, because he obviously meant his late wife.

Not her.

CHAPTER TWELVE

HAZEL FINISHED HER operative report on Sandra Patterson's cervical cerclage as fast as she could. It had been a long time since she'd done a report like this, but it all came back to her quickly.

She made sure that Sandra was settled in the postoperative unit and was comfortable and gave instructions to the residents and nurses who were monitoring her, asking them to page her or Caleb if there was any change.

She grabbed a quick bite to eat, because she hadn't eaten since they came back from Seattle.

Not that she was going to be doing anything else now.

All she had to do was change and go home, but first she was going to see Lizzie and check on her for a final time before she went home.

As she walked through the postoperative wing, she saw that Caleb was in the waiting room. He was back in his street clothes. The white sleeves of his dress shirt were rolled to his elbows, and his hair was still mussed. There were large bags under his eyes, but he was resting.

As if he knew that she was watching, he looked up.

Their gazes locked and her heart skipped a bea,t and her eyes filled with tears.

He nodded encouragingly.

Hazel returned the nod and left to him to his thoughts.

She didn't know what his plans were next or if he had forgiven her for not telling him about Lizzie's pregnancy, but he'd made it clear he was on her birthing center's side. That meant so much.

When she went into the room, Lizzie was lying there, looking pale.

"Hazel!" Lizzie said brightly. "I wasn't sure if you were coming again."

"I wanted to say good-night," Hazel said, stroking Lizzie's hair through the scrub cap that they had put on her. "I wanted to check up on you, see if you needed anything."

"Thanks for being here for me." Lizzie took her hand. "I finally talked to my dad."

"I'm so glad."

"He isn't going to murder Derek. He gave his blessing for us to get married when we graduate."

Hazel smiled. "I'm glad."

"I'm nervous how Derek will feel," Lizzie said. "About the baby."

"You don't have to be nervous about anything. If he loves you, you will be all that matters and he'll mourn with you."

Lizzie squeezed her hand. "Dad has been having a great time with you the last couple of weeks."

"He's a good friend."

Lizzie grinned, but it was the kind of grin that was kind of dopey as the painkillers started to kick in. "Couldn't you be more than friends? It would be cool to have you as a…a mom."

Then Lizzie drifted off.

Hazel's stomach twisted in a knot, and she fought back the tears.

I'd like that too, but your dad doesn't trust me anymore.

She straightened her spine and wiped the tears away as she headed to the doctors' lounge. On her way there she bumped into Timothy Russell, and he didn't look pleased.

"I thought you'd be gone by now."

"I'm sure you'd like that, but you know that it's actually hurting your hospital not letting midwives have privileges. It looks petty. Just thought I would make that clear. The Pattersons are leaving."

"Doubtful. St. Raymond's is the best," Timothy said, but she could see the worry in his face.

"Ask the Pattersons. You take away their right to the health care team they've requested, and they'll walk. That's an awful lot of PR and money your board will lose. Think they'll like that?" Hazel asked smugly.

"Are you threatening me?" Timothy asked furiously.

"No. Just telling you because you know and I know there will be a vote of no confidence in you if word gets out how you treat midwives here at St. Raymond's."

Timothy said nothing, but stormed away.

Victor came around the corner, smiling at her. "I heard that."

Hazel chuckled. "Did you?"

"I did." He grinned. "You're smart, Hazel Rees. I like you."

Hazel nodded. "Thank you, Dr. Anderson."

"You're welcome and please, call me Victor." He headed off down the hall.

Hazel swallowed the lump in her throat. All her emotions were overtaking her. She was exhausted.

She needed some space and distance.

You need Caleb.

She pushed that thought away.

Caleb glanced at the clock on the wall.

There were certain things that people did in the waiting room while waiting for loved ones. His thing was apparently this, watching a hand seemingly go backward around a wall clock.

This was what he'd done when Lizzie was having her surgery.

Now he was waiting for Derek to come and he hoped the young man did. Although, there was still a part of him that wanted to throttle him because he'd impregnated his teenage daughter.

Derek came rushing into the waiting room, panicked.

"Dr. Norris, is Lizzie…"

"She's okay. I'll take you to her."

It was up to Lizzie to tell him about the baby.

Caleb let him into the room and Derek hesitated. He could see the pain on the young man's face.

"It'll be fine," Caleb said. "She needs you."

Derek nodded and went to her side. Caleb watched as Lizzie broke the news to Derek, who held her as she cried.

Their shared grief made his heart hurt, but Derek stayed with Lizzie and it was clear they were in love.

He envied them.

Why envy them? Do something about it. You can have love too.

He wanted more.

But right now, he had to think about Lizzie and the next steps on the road to her recovery.

Derek came out. "I'm going to get some water."

"Everything will be okay," Caleb said.

Derek smiled. "I know. I'm just glad she's here. I love her, Dr. Norris."

"I know you do. And please call me Caleb."

Derek nodded. "Thanks. She'd like to see you. She's a bit groggy."

"Thanks."

He went over to Lizzie's bed. She'd fallen asleep again.

Caleb nodded slowly and touched his daughter's pale face. She looked so small and fragile in that big hospital bed. Yet Lizzie was stronger than he thought.

She was stronger than him.

He had been foregoing love because he didn't want to hurt her. He'd been holding back his grief for the same reason. He'd wanted to protect her just like he'd promised Jane he would. Then Lizzie had said she'd dreamed about her late mother telling her to take care of him.

Lizzie was so worried about him being alone.

Which he was.

He was a fool.

"Hazel Rees is quite impressive. I've thought that all day. She should've been a surgeon," Victor remarked quietly, coming into Lizzie's room.

"Why do you say that?" Caleb asked. "Midwives are just as important as surgeons."

"That's not what I mean. Hazel thinks three steps ahead."

"She's an excellent midwife."

Victor nodded. "I wish she was on my staff."

"Does this hospital respect her though?" Caleb asked. "They don't seem to."

"We're working on it. Timothy Russell is in deep trouble with the other members of the board. I don't think he'll be around much longer. The new vice chair is more sympathetic to the vision of St. Raymond's that all the staff share."

"Working on it isn't good enough," Caleb said. "Victor, I have…"

The chief of staff took a step back. "You're leaving, aren't you?"

"Perhaps it's time I formed my own practice."

Victor smiled with approval. "I'd hate to lose you though."

"You're a good chief, but I need to start running my own life. I need to live. I need a new start and a fresh challenge."

Victor nodded. "Let me know when you're ready to talk this through further."

He left and Caleb glanced down at his daughter. He'd meant what he said about needing a fresh start. He'd never really grieved Jane fully. He'd never let her go. All these years, he'd used work to act as a buffer to keep all these feelings away.

He was numb.

Caleb sat down in the chair next to Lizzie's bed, and tears stung his eyes.

It all came out.

The pain, the loss.

It erupted out of him.

He'd been going through the motions for so many years he wasn't exactly sure how to live again. All those dreams he and Jane had shared, all the chances he'd been to afraid to take suddenly seemed possible again, and it was overwhelming.

Looking at Lizzie, who was stronger than he thought, more resilient than he gave her credit for, was begging him to return to the land of the living. When he'd met Hazel, he'd resented the board of directors for making him deal with such a headstrong, fiery woman.

It was that stubborn woman who'd breathed life back into him.

Things were going to change.

Maybe he'd blown it with Hazel, and he'd live with those consequences if that were the case, but he wasn't going to live in fear anymore. He was going to try.

"Dad?" Lizzie murmured, rousing and wincing.

He reached out and took her hand. "I'm here, sweetie."

"Where's Derek?"

"Gone for water. He'll be back." The postanesthesia care unit nurse popped her head around the door and he motioned for her to come over. She checked on Lizzie and gave her some more morphine.

"You'll feel better soon," Caleb said.

Lizzie nodded, but didn't open her eyes all the way.

"Is Hazel still here?" Lizzie asked groggily.

"No."

His daughter frowned. "I wish you'd see sense."

"What're you talking about?"

Lizzie opened her eyes. "Come on, Dad. You love her."

It shocked him. How did she know?

It's the sedatives. People are always loopy out of surgery.

Except he didn't think so.

"Okay then," he chuckled softly.

"Dad, you're blind. She totally loves you too."

"How about you concentrate on healing?"

Lizzie nodded and drifted back to sleep. Now was not the time to get into it, but Lizzie wasn't wrong.

When she was awake and not drugged up on painkillers, then he could talk to her about what to do. Maybe Lizzie would have some ideas on how to rectify the situation he was in.

Maybe she could help him figure out how to get Hazel to forgive him, because he wanted her in his life.

He wanted them all to be a family.

CHAPTER THIRTEEN

Three weeks later

HAZEL STARED OUT the window of her office, watching the rain fall. She pulled her cardigan around herself tighter. At least the cold snap was over now that summer had officially begun, and despite the rain today, they'd had a couple weeks of sunshine.

She was enjoying the summer warmth, especially after several years of living in southern Arizona.

It had been three weeks since she'd last been at St. Raymond's. She wanted to go and check on Lizzie and Caleb, but she also wanted to give them their space. She had pushed Caleb away, so it was her own fault.

When she and Mark had finished, she didn't remember feeling this kind of pain and longing. She'd just picked herself up and carried on, because she had done the right thing and walked away from him.

So why was it so sore and tender?

Why was it so lonely without Caleb here?

Because you love him.

It was like Caleb had disappeared off the map.

There was a knock on her office door and Bria poked her head in. "Feeling any better?"

"What do you mean? I'm feeling fine."

Bria cocked her eyebrow and came into her office, shutting the door behind her. She joined Hazel at the window. "Come on, be straight with me. I know a lovelorn look when I see it. Remember, I've been through heartbreak before."

"So have I."

"Don't get mad, but I don't think that you have," Bria said, defensively putting up her hands.

"What're you talking about? What about Mark?"

"He was scum," Bria said bluntly. "But I don't think that you were in love with him the same way you are with Caleb."

Hazel swallowed the lump in her throat. "Really? I'm in love with him?"

"Why are you denying it to me? I can read you like a book," Bria said.

Hazel smiled, her lips quivering. "You're right. I love him. I'm in love with him, but I think I ruined everything."

Bria put her arm around her, and Hazel leaned her head against her friend's shoulder. "I don't think you've ruined it at all, Hazel. I believe in love."

"Do you?" Hazel asked sardonically.

"Okay, well, maybe not for me, but I believe in love for others."

Hazel chuckled. "You're such a weirdo."

"Thanks. So tell me what happened in Seattle. You didn't say much when you got back."

Hazel sighed, because just thinking about that

time in Seattle brought back all the memories she'd tried so hard to forget. The sensation of his strong arms around her, his kisses and the way he'd made her feel the best she ever had, because she was so in love with him.

"Caleb and I made love," she admitted.

Bria's eyes widened. "And you don't think that he cares for you?"

"Some men just want to get laid."

"And you think Caleb is like that?"

"No."

Hazel felt foolish. Caleb was not that type of man at all. She knew that the first moment he took her in his arms. Caleb was so different from Mark. She could see it now. When she was first attracted to Caleb, she'd questioned why she always fell for the wrong man.

Only this time she hadn't, and she'd ruined it anyways. She missed him.

Missed their talks.

She missed how easy it was to fall into a conversation with him.

She missed his smile, his laugh and how safe she felt in his arms.

Tears welled in her eyes and she began to cry. Like a fool.

She'd ruined everything.

They both had with their stubbornness.

Bria pulled her into an embrace and just held her for a few minutes.

"Sorry," Hazel said, sniffling. "We got into a fight. He blamed me for not telling him about his daughter. I blamed him being taken off the Patterson case, when it wasn't him."

"That's nonsense. If Caleb doesn't understand patient confidentiality, then he's an idiot."

"I don't think we can work together anymore. Him and me that is."

"You're both professionals, and if he can't see that, he wasn't the right one for you."

"The thing is, I think he is."

Bria sighed. "You're just as prideful and stubborn as he is."

"I suppose so."

"You need to go tell him how you feel. It's scary, but don't let him slip away. Trust me when I tell you that if you find love, don't let it go so easily."

They hugged again.

"I'll go see him tonight and try to make it right. Or at least I'll know the answer and not keep worrying about it."

"Right. You have a meeting with a new tenant, by the way," Bria said. "For that office space we're renting out to help fund our center."

"I do?"

Joan knocked on the door and stuck her head in. "Sorry for interrupting, but Hazel this package just came in from St. Raymond's."

Bria and Hazel exchanged surprised glances.

"Do you know what it is?" Hazel asked.

"No idea." Bria got an alert and looked at her phone. "Oh, shoot, one of my patients has gone into labor. Fill me in later about what's in the package."

Hazel nodded. "Thanks, Bria."

Her friend blew her a kiss and left.

Hazel took the package from Joan and opened it.

It was a letter from Dr. Victor Anderson with an offer of a closer working relationship between their clinic and the hospital, in particular, for Hazel. The chairman of the board, or rather the new one, had also written her a letter of apology.

Hazel was floored.

It was starting to pay off. This was what she'd devoted all her time to. She was so proud of her and Bria's clinic. It had filled a need for a long time, but there was now a part of her that wanted more than just work in her life.

She wanted good talks about books, laughter and pumpkin pie.

She wanted to be a part of Lizzie's life, more than as just her midwife, and she wanted Caleb.

And maybe a child of her own.

Her alarm went off and she cursed under her breath. She tucked the contract away.

She was glad for the privileges at St. Raymond's.

She collected what she needed and headed downstairs to meet the prospective new doctor who wanted to set up a practice. Joan had booked it, Bria had arranged it and now Hazel was going to meet the doctor.

Hazel unlocked the empty space they planned to rent out and waited.

The door opened behind her and she turned around. Her breath caught in her throat.

"Caleb? What're you doing here?"

He smiled and glanced around. "I had an appointment to see this new rental space."

"Why? You already have an office at the hospital."

"Not for long. I'm forming my own private practice. I have to work out my notice period yet, so my practice will build slowly."

"You are?"

"Yes." He took a step closer to her.

"But... You're head of obstetrics at St. Raymond's."

"Was."

"Was?"

"I quit."

"You quit?"

"I'm following a dream I had that I put on hold because I was too afraid to take a risk while raising a young child. I was numb. You inspired me though."

"I inspired you?"

"You opened the Women's Health Center. You took a chance and followed your dreams."

"Yes. I suppose I did. I'm surprised St. Raymond's offered an apology for Timothy's behavior and a promise to work with Bria and me more closely. I thought that had been your doing, but not if you've handed in your notice."

"No. Not my doing. Victor was impressed with you."

"And were you?"

"Yes. I am." Caleb smiled at her and took another step closer to her.

Her heart skipped a beat, her body trembling. "You are?"

"Yes. I'm sorry for what happened with Timothy taking you off Sandra's case. I had nothing to do with that."

"I know and I'm sorry that I overreacted. I've just… I'm so used to being let down and hurt." A tear slipped down her cheek.

"And I'm sorry for lashing out at you about Lizzie. I was scared for her, that's all. I know you couldn't tell me about the pregnancy."

"I would never, ever harm her intentionally."

"I know that." Caleb reached up and wiped the tear away with the pad of his thumb. "Hazel, I've been numb for so long. You breathed life back into me. I fell in love with you."

"Fell? Like past tense?" she teased, her body melting as she gazed up into his blue-gray twinkling eyes.

"Not past tense. I am in love with you, Hazel, and I want to be with you. Only you. I've been afraid of love for so long, afraid of losing again and having my heart broken, but you give me the strength to want to try again. You brought me back to life." He stroked her cheek and then leaned in to kiss her.

She didn't have to say anything and just melted into his arms.

Melted into his kiss.

Caleb savored the feeling of Hazel's lips against his. It had taken all of his courage to tell her how he had been feeling. He had been planning this moment for three weeks. Once Lizzie was stable, she had actually helped him plan this and got Bria in on it.

He'd wanted to make a grand gesture to let Hazel know how much she meant to him. Even though he'd be running his own practice, he'd also be able to work closely with Hazel and consult with her whenever she needed him. He wasn't sure how it was going to go, but he was willing to put his heart on the line for her, and Lizzie was thrilled with the prospect that Hazel could be joining their family.

It had been so long since he had been in love.

Since he opened his heart, but this was what he was waiting for.

He was waiting for Hazel.

Seeing her standing there in the empty rental space took his breath away. Three weeks was too long for them to be apart. He'd missed her.

Completely.

And when he'd entered the room, all he could do was stare at her for a few moments. He was remembering each inch of her. The silken feel of her skin, the way her hair felt between his fingers.

The way she tasted.

She was everything he wanted.

His thorn.

Hazel wrapped her arms around him. Her dark eyes were full of tears, but she was smiling up at him.

"We both overreacted, and then Lizzie lost the baby and…it took me a long time to process. Can you forgive me for taking so long?"

"Only if you can forgive me for being so stubborn too," she said, leaning her head against his chest.

"Deal."

She smiled at him, the dimple showing up on her cheek, and he bent over and lightly kissed her on the lips. "I love you, Hazel."

"I love you too, Caleb. So much, it's kind of terrifying because I didn't think that I would ever fall in love again, but then I realized that I hadn't actually been in love before. So I guess I didn't think that I would ever really fall in love like this."

"Will you marry me, Hazel? Lizzie and I want you to be a part of your family."

"Yes! That sounds wonderful. Of course when you marry me, the both of you will be dragged into my big, spread out family."

"Lizzie would love that."

"She might change her mind when she meets

some of my nieces and nephews," Hazel muttered. "So, are you still serious about opening a practice here?"

He looked around the small rental space. "Of course, why wouldn't I?"

"You want to work so close to your wife?" she asked, cocking an eyebrow. "We didn't exactly always see eye to eye when we first met."

"And I'm sure we'll have plenty more to discuss, but yes, this is what I want. For now. There is always the possibility that we could both sell our practices and eventually move up to Alaska."

Hazel grinned. "My parents would like that, but I think that's way off. I just started the Women's Health Center here with Bria. I'm not leaving quite yet."

"Okay, in a few years maybe?"

"Maybe," Hazel agreed.

They kissed again and then walked out of the building hand in hand.

"So, I suppose I have to call your father up and ask for permission?" Caleb asked.

"Yes, and I'm going to have to go see Lizzie and ask for her permission."

Caleb chuckled. "She's already expecting you to pay her a visit."

"Oh?"

"She's at home, and she's having her fiancé, Derek, make dinner." They stopped in front of Caleb's car and he opened the door for her.

"I suppose we need to stop by the bakery and get another pie."

"Why?" Caleb asked.

"I have to butter her up somehow," Hazel joked.

"I suppose we can stop at the bakery and get a pumpkin pie."

"And a chocolate pie too," Hazel said. "I've been craving one of those chocolate pies this last week."

Caleb laughed and shut the door. He climbed into the driver's seat and glanced over at Hazel, who was smiling back at him. He was the luckiest man in the world, and he had almost been too stubborn and let her slip right through his fingers.

He was glad that he was able to finally get his head on straight.

He was glad that he was no longer numb and that he could finally breathe again.

For the first time in a long time, he was alive and he was glad to be alive. He had a lot to be thankful for.

He'd had to deal with the thorn in his side, and he'd been pricked by that thorn and fallen in love just like a kind of crazy fairy tale.

He had found his happily-ever-after with his beautiful rose.

EPILOGUE

Six months later

IT WAS COLD out and snow was falling.

The park service warned them that the path to the Benson Bridge would be too icy to traverse, and that was fine. Hazel just wanted their wedding picture to be taken in front of the falls; she didn't have to be in front of the bridge.

Bria had tried to convince her to wait until the spring or summer to get married, but Hazel hadn't wanted to wait that long. They had been together long enough. She was tired of waiting.

She honestly couldn't wait that long anyway, because in the early autumn she was due to give birth.

Hazel still couldn't believe what had happened the last time they'd had a night to themselves. She had been on the pill, but it was not infallible and right before she was about to walk down the aisle to marry the man of her dreams, she'd just peed on a stick and discovered that she was going to have a baby.

She was staring at the plus sign in disbelief.

"Well?" Bria asked.

"It's positive," Hazel said in shock.

"Well, that's wonderful!"

"It is."

It was everything that Hazel had always dreamed of, but she and Caleb had plans and a baby wasn't part of those plans right now. What was she going to tell him?

"Do you want me to get him?" Bria asked.

"It's bad luck to see the bride before the wedding," Hazel said automatically.

"Oh, come on, it's not that bad." Bria got up and put on her parka over her simple bridesmaid dress. "You have to tell him."

Hazel nodded. "Yes, it's going to distract me for the whole service if I don't tell him."

"I'll send him in."

Bria disappeared and Hazel stared at the stick again.

Everyone would be arriving to the Multnomah Falls lodge where they were having their wedding. It was a small wedding, but a lot of her family had managed to fly in, despite the winter weather. She didn't want to delay the service any longer than she had to, but she had to see Caleb and tell him the news.

She was kicking herself that she hadn't seen the signs, herself, earlier.

She was a midwife, after all.

Caleb didn't see them either and he's an obstetrician.

Caleb walked into the bridal change room and he looked concerned, but then his gaze raked over her body in a way that made her tremble.

"You're absolutely stunning."

Hazel blushed. "Thanks."

Then his eyes fell to the stick that she was still holding in her hands and he paled. "Is that…is that a pregnancy test?"

She nodded. "I'm pregnant."

Caleb didn't say anything at first, and she began to panic.

"I know it's not part of our immediate plans, but I'm pregnant and I'm pretty happy about it. Shocked, but happy."

Caleb pulled her up into his arms and held her. "I'm happy too. I guess I'm a little shocked as well. When did it happen?"

"That night when we both were off duty and Lizzie had moved in with Derek. The night in the living room, remember?" she teased.

He grinned. "That would make sense."

"I can't believe I didn't notice my symptoms sooner."

"Ditto." He reached down and touched her belly. "I'm really thrilled, Hazel. Another child."

"Do you think that Lizzie will be okay with this? She'll be nineteen years older than the baby."

"Are you kidding? She wants a brother or a sister. She'd gladly take one of each."

"One of each!" Hazel fake swooned and then set down the pregnancy test. She wrapped her arms around his neck.

"It would be perfect."

Hazel cocked an eyebrow. "Perfect, eh?"

"Your parents will be thrilled to have another grandchild."

"Grandchildren," Hazel corrected him. "They have already claimed Lizzie as one of theirs."

He smiled. "Yes. That means so much to me."

"You mean so much to me." She reached up and kissed him. The kiss deepened as his hands went around her, pulling her flush against his body.

"Why don't we skip the wedding?" he murmured in her ear, nibbling down her neck in a way that made her blood heat.

"No. We can't do that. Everyone flew in to see us get married. We have to go do that."

Caleb groaned. "I suppose, but I feel a bit put out. You're so gorgeous. I just want to carry you off to bed."

"You can do that later," she said with a smile. "You might as well get it while you can. Soon I'm going to be too big."

"That won't stop me," Caleb whispered.

"You're awful." Except that she was so in love with him. Everything he said or did thrilled her, and she was incredibly happy right now. She was getting the family she'd always wanted. She had Lizzie as a great daughter and now she was secretly hoping for a boy, but she didn't care either way as long the baby was healthy.

Everything was working out right.

She was never one to believe in fairy tales or

happily-ever-afters and she certainly didn't believe in Prince Charmings, but somehow the one man that she sworn she had to resist was her knight in shining armor after all.

The man who drove her crazy, who'd grated on her nerves the first time she'd met him and who now drove her wild with passion. The man she loved more than anything else, and he was finally going to be her husband.

"We better go." Caleb sighed. "The ceremony is about to start."

"Yes, but I do have one more thing to show you."

He cocked an eyebrow. "Oh, and what's that?"

She lifted her dress slightly and showed him what she was wearing underneath, in particular on her feet. It wasn't glass slippers, but she knew he would like it all the same.

"Rainbow toe socks," he chuckled.

"The source of my power. Like I said."

"You did say that, and I hope that you wear them in bed tonight."

Hazel laughed and took his hand as they headed out into the lodge to join their families legally.

Their hearts were already joined.

A family forever.

* * * * *

*Look out for the next story in the
Portland Midwives duet*

The Midwife from His Past
by Julie Danvers

*If you enjoyed this story, check out these
other great reads from Amy Ruttan*

**A Ring for His Pregnant Midwife
Reunited with Her Surgeon Boss
Falling for His Runaway Nurse**

All available now!